Sherry

Thought you might enjoy the latest classic. Probably not your cup of tea but I think you'll enjoy the human touches. A bit of WWII history, my fiction and bits from my childhood.

Hope you enjoy!

Bob Owen

July 19, 2011

Also by Bob Guess:

Waiting for the Green Flash

The Plastic Princess

Hey Mister, How's Your Sister?
(children's book)

Kumpel

Bob Guess

iUniverse, Inc.
Bloomington

Kumpel

iUniverse books may be ordered through booksellers or by contacting:

iUniverse
1663 Liberty Drive
Bloomington, IN 47403
www.iuniverse.com
1-800-Authors (1-800-288-4677)

ISBN: 978-1-4620-2272-4 (sc)
ISBN: 978-1-4620-2273-1 (hc)
ISBN: 978-1-4620-2274-8 (ebook)

Printed in the United States of America

iUniverse rev. date:06/15/2011

For Buddy (1923–1959)
USMC
Okinawa, Guam, Guadalcanal, Peleliu, Emirau, Korea

ACKNOWLEDGEMENTS

NEARLY A HALF MILLION enemy soldiers were held in prison camps scattered around the United States during World War II. Information about their internment was a difficult topic for research. The combatants in that Great War, both Allied and Axis, are passing at an accelerated pace, one source citing a thousand deaths a day of American veterans of the war alone. Materials on the prison camps are dated and there have been few follow-ups in the last forty years. Understandably, the subject of enemy prisoners has not been a popular American theme for literature and film, in contrast to the dozens of novels and movies on American captives from *King Rat* to *Deer Hunter* to a more recent *Rescue Dawn*.

My interest in the subject was a childhood acquisition that occurred as I watched enemy POWs working in the fields and alongside the roads of the small Texas town where I grew up. What was the sheer unlikelihood of their walking off the newsreel screens into my small world? I have since learned a great deal about what was happening to those men when they returned each evening to their camp. In the writing and research I have tried to never forget that those were men who had taken the lives of many Americans' loved ones. Separating deed, cause, and responsibility was a challenging conundrum.

A number of good people helped me with this book, providing research, recollections, and encouragement. I would start with Mr. Google, whose depth of knowledge is amazing, always there to augment the hardback histories, the e-mails, letters, and personal interviews which form the bulk of the factual information contained in the story.

Gunter Langen and Hortz Steidi were prisoners in camps much like Camp 67, though neither was in Texas. Both these men came back to America after the war and settled into a life in this country. I appreciate their sharing first-hand memories with me.

Julian Harkness was a teenager working on a farm with prisoners much like J.T. in the novel. I was sorely tempted to use a story he cheerfully recalled to me. A car loaded with teenagers, including Mr. Harkness, went out of control and crashed into the main gate of the POW camp near his Arizona hometown. Armed guards swept down on them, ready to repel a breakout of prisoners. He recalled being terrified. Regretfully, Mr. Harkness passed away before the publishing of this book.

My thanks to the Bonehead Boys of Childress, Texas, a fraternal group in existence for over sixty years. Their recollections of the Army Air Force base and the POW camp near Childress were very helpful. Several responded to my seeking of information: Jarvis Michie, Joe Powell, Crews Bell, Troy Boykin, Fred Herrin, Leo Sims, and Harry Trueblood. Other "boys" included Everette Groseclose, whose father built bombing targets at the base. Of German descent, Everette recalls the family's need to always be quick to demonstrate their alliance to the U.S., lest they be thought of as sympathizers. He gave a chilling account of his father and other armed men piling into two pickups to go out and search for prisoners who were rumored to have escaped.

Jon Bennett observed prisoners working at the cotton compress in town. He remembers them as pleasant and agreeable. Jon was kind enough to provide other research for my project.

Jay Sharp remembers seeing prisoners on the base and discussing their possible escape with his parents. They questioned the geographical enormity of such an attempt.

Charles Villyard tells of watching skip bombing on the lake as the planes dropped sand-filled bombs at a floating target. Max Taylor remembers the airmen of the base and their impact on the small town, especially the young women, several of whom married men stationed there. And Delbert Trew was able to give me helpful information on the medical treatment of prisoners at Camp McLean and the fact that captured German doctors worked in tandem with the American physicians there.

Joanie Sailer was on board early in the creation of *Kumpel*, providing important connections to interviewees and remaining in touch and support throughout. Thanks to Bob Simon for valuable leads, to Steve Craig of the Childress County Heritage Museum, and to Christopher Blelloch, a fledgling engineer who gave Chapter 33 a sense of reality.

A special thanks to M.Sgt. Alfred Page, USAF (Ret.), who held forth on World War II planes and bombing procedures from his hospital bed in October. M.Sgt. Page passed away four months later.

Thanks to Gloria Laube, who has patiently provided editing and manuscript preparation for all my books.

I am grateful to have been able to obtain the help of Monika Stimpert. An enormous *danke schön* to Monika for her German translations and insights into the German culture. The subject of POWs was not new to Monika. Her father was captured and held in Leningrad by the Russians from 1945 to 1947.

And last but not least Ellen Conner for the fine cover design.

Thank you all.

On a warm Texas Monday in June, Jerome Thayer (J.T.) Graham, fresh from his ninth year of schooling, began his summer job on the Ed McConnell farm. Less than ten miles away, a dusty vehicle pulled into POW Camp 67 and deposited its lone passenger, Obersturmführer Werner von Hoffmann, the first SS officer to be sent to the camp. Neither event was newsworthy, but the day that followed was monumental. On Tuesday, June 6, 1944, a massive invasion force of allied troops landed on the beaches of Normandy. On Wednesday, soldiers and airmen gathered outside the double barbed wire fence of the prison camp and waved newspapers with the headlines: **INVASION! Allied Troops Land in France! The Invasion Is On—First Wave Hits Omaha Beach! D-Day!** The prisoners, who had been a passive group prior to von Hoffmann's arrival, protested harassment and refused to go to their jobs on the base or board the trucks for farm work details. Base Commander Colonel Mitchell Payne responded by serving the POWs biscuits and water for their lunch and repeated the menu for the evening meal. When the prisoners refused to work again on Thursday, the colonel substituted sliced white bread with no change in the drink list. On Friday, the German prisoners returned to their jobs.

Chapter 1

OBERSTURMFÜHRER WERNER VON HOFFMANN walked slowly from one end of the troop barracks to the other, slapping his glove in one hand and staring down each of the prisoners who stood at attention by their bunks. Otto Becker was one of the few watching who knew that the glove slapping was a custom of the true Junkers, the caste that had produced most German generals for centuries. Was von Hoffmann a Junker or was this just another act of intimidation for those present? Unlike most of the troops from the lines, who arrived in tattered uniforms, von Hoffmann's was relatively intact, including the lightening bolts of the SS. Prisoners were allowed to wear their uniforms on weekends or special occasions, but most had long since been discarded or awaited some future repair. Von Hoffman was a small man of light musculature with a head too large for his body. His eyes were set deep, the skin around them dark, his mouth a thin line that seemed lipless.

"German soldiers," von Hoffmann began, "must resist the Americans who enslave us here. We cannot confront them militarily, at this time, but we must make their job more and more difficult. They must know we are members of the greatest army in the history of the world and that ultimately we will prevail over all nations who oppose us. The work stoppage was the first message to those who think us cowering prisoners. We are solders of the Reich and we will demonstrate so again and again. The so-called newspapers the Americans were gloating about were nothing more than propaganda, meant to destroy your fighting spirit and break you into slobbering slaves. Anyone can print a newspaper headline and wave it in your face. And the two radios you have broadcast propaganda as well, and it is good you cannot understand it. Listen to their inane music, if you must. I will be asking the colonel in command for German music at a later time. So, once again, you must slow your work production, refuse their advances of friendship, protest and contest *everything!* Understood?"

"And shall we ask for a better quality of bread and perhaps ice in the water next time, Lieutenant?" Otto Becker asked in his strong bass voice.

The room became as still as death, as the other prisoners looked out of the corners of their eyes to see, to witness, what would surely be a fierce dressing down, at the least.

Von Hoffmann walked to where Otto stood. He looked up at the tall soldier and presented his best sneer.

"And your name, *Private?*"

"Private Otto Becker, sir."

And that is, Private, German Army, Becker, is it not?"

"Private Otto, Prisoner of War, Becker, sir."

"Are you questioning my decision to refuse work those two days, Becker?"

"It's more a matter of clarifying an alternate path we might follow as prisoners in the United States, Lieutenant. I've been here a few months, others in other camps for a year. The Americans are slovenly followers of the Geneva Convention. They feed us well, they give us medical treatment, the Red Cross is allowed access to each of our soldiers, and that provides an outlet for any grievance we might have. We are treated well. To bring punishment on ourselves is counterproductive. We basically have two choices. One is to get by as comfortably as we can until our troops defeat the Allies, invade and conquer England, then come to America and free us. The other choice is to escape."

"Ah ha, now the Becker name becomes clear to me. You are der Verrückt Otto. The Americans call you 'Crazy Otto.'"

"Yes, sir."

"And that's because you tried to escape?"

"No, I did *not* try to escape. Escape from Camp 67 would be folly. You saw this country, this state, when you came in didn't you, Obersturmführer? It is endless. We are six hundred miles from the nearest port, three hundred miles from Mexico, and would you find one American between here and Mexico who would aid your escape? Along with the miles, there are thousands of hostile people."

"Thank you for the geography lesson, Private. I will decide what is folly and what is strategy. You will do as I say."

"Captain Müeller has been in charge, sir. Has that changed?"

"Obviously it has, Becker. What hasn't changed is the punishment for disrespect to an officer. You are on notice."

"I have served my country well, Obersturmführer. I will do so in the future, but don't ask us to be prisoners in a jail, inside a jail. Am I to look over one shoulder for an American guard with a loaded weapon and over the other for my comrades who wish to impose another sentence on me?"

"I think you have just given yourself good advice, Becker. It would be wise to follow it." Von Hoffmann fixed a steady gaze into Becker's eyes, waiting for further insubordination, but Otto said nothing. "I understand you are one of the five soldiers who speak English, Becker. I will have duties for you in that respect." Hoffmann wheeled from Otto, clicked his heels, and said, "Troops are dismissed. Heil Hitler!"

Chapter 2

THEIR LINES HAD BEEN pounded for five straight hours with no sign of letup. Tank fire, artillery, bombers, strafing fighters, infantry snipers, every armament known to the North Africa campaign had been assembled to shell the Afrika Korps front line in what could only mean a major Allied push was to follow. The Germans had not yet retreated but were paying a terrible price to hold this patch of desert that seemed to be important, though no different than the arid terrain a hundred miles any direction from the battle. The Germans were a thrown-together division-and-a-half consisting of parts of other panzer divisions which had been destroyed or seriously depleted. That 88mm anti-aircraft guns were being used against tanks was illustrative of the desperate position in which Rommel's army found itself. Out of gas, both literally and figuratively, one more brilliant tactical surprise seemed beyond Rommel's resources.

They knew he was there. Bullets and shell fragments kept kicking up sand that landed on his helmet and face. Otto wiped the grit from his eyes and tried to make a plan. If he raised his head, he was a dead man, and if he stood and ran he was even an easier target. He had watched Bach disintegrate in his hole fifty feet away when a mortar round landed in his lap. Karl Bach, who had been an engaging eighteen-year-old recruit minutes before, had bragged of his composer ancestor but claimed he was more the recipient of genes from his mother's side, which had been heavy with warriors. Bach had lasted four days in the desert.

Otto's first plan, aside from standing and taking on a Brit tank, was to crawl back toward the light armored line hoping the smoke and dust, both getting thicker by the minute, might give him some cover. He turned his head and looked back at armor. They were moving back. They were retreating! No word to the damned infantry squads. How the hell did the Brits close so fast? That was the way Rommel charged, not the Brit bastard Montgomery! He *had* to look out before he retreated. He thought of holding his helmet to the right to draw fire while he looked. He'd seen that in some old movie. Maybe the Brits had seen it, too. *If you must die, don't die stupid, Otto.* He began to edge his eyes above the wall of his pathetic dugout fortress. A cruiser tank had stopped its track two feet from his head, poised like before a fly swatter is snapped to a fly. Death by the tank track flashed through his mind. Would they find his remains? Thousands had died in this desert and had been buried in graves that probably no longer existed, covered by the ghibli-driven sands and the endless movement of vehicles in this yo-yo campaign. Advance, fall back, encircle. It was madness. How many times had El Alamein alone been attacked, or taken or lost. He couldn't remember.

Two Aussie soldiers with rifles and fixed bayonets looked down at him.

"Three choices, Jerry," the red-haired one said. "We stick ya like the pig ya is, we shoot ya, or me mate in the funny tin can makes a road out ya face."

"He don't understand nothin', Harry. He's a Hun Kraut. Do we give him the fourth choice, Harry? Us follow him with our bayonets up his ass to the prisoner compound."

Otto understood every word. His war was over. He knew that the only decision to make was whether to die right here in this miserable hole or try surrendering.

"Easier to roll him down, mate. Save a bullet. Yeah, we're talking about you, boogerface, and don't look at me when I talk. Get yer head down and your hands up!"

Otto raised his hands.

"He understood you, Harry! I'll be damned. You speak the English, Jerry?"

"Yes," said Otto.

"Shit, better take him back, Harry. He might tell them something."

"Yeah, like we're gettin' our arse kicked. Information like that."

"One fucking Kraut ain't worth gettin' in trouble for, ya know. Let's take him back, maybe get a tinnie while we're there."

"Yeah, and supposing we walk all the way back there, there's no tinnie of beer and blooming officers everywhere so we can't shoot him. Waste of time, mate."

"Harry, the cruiser is pushing on, there's mates everywhere would see us finish him now. He's gotta go back, Harry."

"All right, all right." Harry poked the bayonet into Otto's chest, penetrating his jacket but bringing no blood. "Okay, Adolph, this way. We're gonna march you through a *real* army."

The two soldiers directed Otto through the litter of war to an area a mile behind the Allied armored line. They were joined on the way by dozens of other prisoners, some of whom Otto recognized by face or insignia. The march was loosely guarded by troops who would have been happy to see them break from the group and run. *Don't die stupid, Otto,* he told himself again. *Do as you're told and watch for a safe way to flee if such an opportunity presents itself.*

He never saw if his two captors got their tinnies of beer for their prisoners. They had arrived at a collection point where trucks were lined up ten deep and were immediately being loaded, filling one truck, then another. The prisoners were told to stand and then shoved tightly against each other in a sardinelike optimum use of space, then the trucks set off in collective roar across the desert.

It was like following the lead dog, eating the thick clouds of dust stirred up by the trucks in front of them. They closed their eyes and covered their faces with their jackets, all the time coughing out wads of wet dirt that dried instantly in their hands.

Several hours later they arrived at a huge compound of German and Italian prisoners guarded by a force so large as to make an escape attempt unwise. They had made but one stop. The truck's bed was urine soaked, and several men had fainted.

At the compound Otto was singled out, along with officers, and taken to tents and questioned. He made no attempt to deny his English skills but was uncooperative and soon was returned to the general prisoner population. British food rations were distributed with water. Water was the most welcome aspect of the issue. Otto had not had water for two days, and then it had been the foul-tasting rations which were delivered in gasoline cans and tasted of both liquids.

Two days later they were transported by truck to a rail line compound. It appeared to hold half the Afrika Korps, thousands of exhausted, wounded, and defeated men. Here rations were even more spare. Each day British trucks and trains hauled away hundreds of prisoners bound for Orion and Casablanca. The truck drivers and guards were frequently angry and vocal about their duty, an army far from the one they had in mind when they joined. Otto was again questioned, denied water and food, then questioned again. From the line of questioning, Otto determined that the interrogators may have thought him an officer in a private's disguise. His tall, proud bearing, intelligent eyes, and square jaw set at a defiant angle said *elite* to most who met him. *What could a private know that would be of use,* he had thought. *I am a waste of time.* The questioning had been intense and humiliating, as well as futile. *All because I have English? Would you like me to cry and say I knew it was over when the new American tanks arrived, Grant and Sherman you called them, our shells bouncing off them like bothersome flies? I kept fighting but I* knew. *There, your interrogation has broken me.*

Otto learned that most of his last division had smashed their rifles and blown up every piece of armor and equipment before being marched away. It was Easter of 1943 and Otto was bound for Casablanca and a fate unknown.

Chapter 3

AT CASABLANCA, OTTO JOINED an entire city of prisoners. The compound covered a hundred acres of the same barren landscape from which they had come. The compound was clean, as much for the sake of the guards as the prisoners. Many of the prisoners had arrived with wounds, malaria, and typhus. Diarrhea or dysentery were a given. Most of the prisoners slept on the ground, the officers occupied the few tents available. Aside from a strict ration of water and British food rations usually given once, sometimes twice a day, the time was spent cleaning the grounds, trying to obtain cigarettes, and exchanging stories of their captures. One day, Otto heard shouting and gunfire at the gate area of the yards. Later he was told that local Arabs had tried to storm the gates, not to free them but to kill as many Germans as possible. The guard unit repelled them, but there were reports of casualties. The Arabs had not truly taken sides during the North African campaign. In the villages, they greeted each army with a mixture of disdain and feigned allegiance as they became the occupier du jour. Historians might conclude they assisted the Allied Armies to a greater degree since the British had experience and history in the region. Perhaps they saw the Allies as the eventual winners and chose sides with the future in mind. Regardless of where their allegiance, if any, was placed, there is little doubt there was Islamic pleasure in seeing two "Christian" armies cut each other into pieces.

One prisoner had been beaten to death the night before by members of his unit who said he was a deserter. Otto was not interviewed again, having been no help to that point. As the Aussie said, "Getting our arse kicked" was the extent of his knowledge as to what went on. They didn't need his take on strategy, either. Rommel was already a legend. Otto had learned two books had already been written on him and his daring maneuvers that had kept the Afrika Korps a military force for months after the troop and equipment numbers of the Allied Forces should have ended it.

There had been no mail delivery for several weeks prior to capture and none at this place called "Prisoner of War Transient Enclosure." He had met another soldier from Dresden, but he had no word of conditions there. Otto hoped his wife and son had gone to Berlin to her family. Though it was likely no safer, at least the four of them might fare better than a woman and a seven-year-old boy alone.

Two weeks went by without the sound of a gun, the drone of a fighter bomber, or a sergeant yelling, "Achtung, get ready!" The change from constant action to the routine of useless boredom had not been easy. Food was short as were tempers, and soldiers, with no enemy available, fought among themselves, cursed the guards, and were generally surly and of a dark mind.

Insects never seen by some enjoyed full camp access, and the flies were so thick they sometimes had to be swallowed with the food. Sleeping outside was not new, but the silence was. He had learned to sleep through the sound of gunfire, now there was none and he lay awake most of the night. The mail issue became a focal point of prisoner complaints. The guards laughed when asked about it. "What you think we are, Fritz, your bloody postie?"

The day the ships came was a welcome one to many. Though no one knew for which port they were to set sail, the change of routine alone was a relief. That relief was tempered by a terrible feeling that this was the *final* surrender. Any illusion of a German Army breakthrough to Casablanca and a rescue of the Afrika Korps was now not even worthy of pipe dream status. The Afrika Korps was no more.

American Liberty ships were not the *Queen Mary*. The *Queen had* been used for one prisoner crossing of five thousand, but the uproar about that use of the grand ship had been Empire-wide. The Liberty ships were plain and had been built somewhat hastily to replace ships sunk by German submarines. Ironically, the ships that picked up prisoners at Casablanca had just disembarked several thousand American troops in England that were to become part of the invasion at Normandy.

The most significant improvement of the prisoners' lot was the food. On the ship they were served three meals of small portions. It was a mixed blessing given the almost immediate onslaught of sea sickness, which, paired with the natural nausea of stomachs adjusting to new and rich foods, made for more misery than had existed at Casablanca.

Prisoners were allowed on deck in areas where there was no lashed-on equipment, but the opportunity for sightseeing was difficult with their heads hung over the rail chumming the fish. Much of the day was spent cleaning up the passenger holds of the prisoners' sickness. Otto was a fortunate one who was neither ill nor seasick. He ate well, having his pick from trays left untouched by troop mates who dashed for the head or rail. The troops ate in two groups, port and starboard, but the division became unnecessary after two days at sea.

The number of guards on board ship seemed small to Otto. However, there was no talk of mutiny or resistance. The sickness had sapped them and many were just happy to be alive and to be distancing themselves, each day, farther from combat. It was to be a long trip, made more so by the maneuvering of the ships to avoid the German submarines who would likely be unaware of their cargo. *Bombed by our allies the Italians, sunk by our own submarines. That would be a fitting end to my crazy war,* thought Otto.

Otto had managed a ground level accommodation of the hammocks stacked three high. It provided quick access, with the downside being seasick occupants of the hammocks above him.

With time on his hands, he contemplated the last three years of his life. He had joined the Germany National Work Service (RAD) to be able to remain at home, near his teaching job, his wife and son. When the army became a choice made for him, he had strived to be the best soldier possible.

It was Otto Franz Becker's infantry skills which had *allowed* him to stay a private. His education qualified him to be an officer or at the least an NCO, but he had no desire to lead, to order, to direct or plan. He was the great salesman who would be wasted in the front office, a sailor transferred to the Sahara, an extraordinary ground fighter who wanted to be responsible only for his life and those he took. Otto led the young soldiers as an example of bravery, a teacher now of a different sort. And so, commanding officers ceased to offer him promotions or commissions and were content to benefit by his production at the front.

Otto's language proficiency allowed him to move freely among those who spoke English or French. From a friendly ship guard, he learned that the prisoners were being shipped to the United States and that almost two hundred thousand German troops had been captured in North Africa alone. The guard didn't know why the United States was the destination but Otto had observed the progressive disorder at the Casablanca compound and knew *that* billet could not be a permanent one. How could perhaps a thousand U.S. and British troops contain a hundred thousand Axis fighters indefinitely when their homeland and army were so near? And why take a thousand troops off the lines to become sitters for the enemy? Relocating Otto and his like made perfect sense to him, but would one prison camp be just like the other? In less than two months, he would find out.

Chapter 4

HAPPY TO PORT, SICK of the sea, the New York Harbor was welcome, though awesome and intimidating. It was the first look for most of the gaunt men who crowded the portholes and deck areas. It was Otto Becker's second. In 1930, during the summer before his first year enrollment at Dresden University's Department of Literature, Culture, and Language, he had traveled to America with his physician father. They had come to visit his father's brother who had emigrated to the German colony in Fredericksburg, Texas, several years before. Although Germany was in an economic depression as severe as any, the doctor was able to manage the trip. He had brushed aside those who had criticized his extravagance, given the times. He felt the political climate which was stirred by street agitation directed toward the sitting government and Jews would only get worse, soon making social travel impossible. His instincts had been right. What the doctor had not anticipated was that the social unrest would be at the direction of a strong man who then would brutally restore order to the riotous streets.

That had been thirteen years before. Otto had only two memories of New York. He remembered the great lady holding a torch as they entered the harbor and he remembered a scene much like home, that of hundreds of men shuffling about the streets looking for work, help, or a handout.

The city seemed unchanged, as intact as its grand statute. Some of the soldiers were puzzled, then became agitated. They had been told that the Luftwaffe had bombed to the ground both the great cities of London and New York. Goebbels had even produced a film that was shown to the troops, showing the leveled city and the toppled statute. Though crudely made, the soldiers had eagerly embraced its message and cheered the success of the proud Nazi military machine. They had discussed the possibility that they would be among the invasion forces sent to America after they finished the desert campaign. Neither the desert nor New York had fulfilled expectations.

In New York, the prisoners were inoculated for different "hygienic" possibilities, deloused, their heads shaved, and they were given a perfunctory physical examination. Those whose uniforms were too tattered to provide cover were issued bits and pieces of American military uniforms, the greater the mismatch the more amusing to the bored clothing personnel. Many of the soldiers rejected the clothing, preferring their battered uniforms instead.

Otto had expected transportation to the prisons to be by boxcar. That's how Allied prisoners had left North Africa bound for German work camps. Instead, a modern train with comfortable seats, toilets, and hot food was provided. Otto thought this must be some sort of setup for the well-known American sense of humor. He imagined the punch line—the train clears the city and the watching eyes of the Red Cross and it would stop. The prisoners would then be forced off the train and made to walk the hundreds of miles to a Stalag work camp where the Americans would exact their pent-up revenge. Before arriving at a camp they would be marched through village streets lined with angry natives who had lost a loved one in the war.

The train left New York, traveled all day and none of his fears were realized. Across the boundless countryside through cities alive with industry, the prisoner train pressed steadily toward the terminus, a flatland called the Texas Panhandle.

Becker had been amazed. He had forgotten the enormity of the country. The nation his country was fighting was unspoiled. No bombed out cities, no visible signs of a people at war. On occasion, when the train stopped to take on food and water he would see men in military uniforms, soldier and sailor, but the cities themselves did not seem to be militarized or concerned with attack. In North Africa he had heard of the bombing of the German cities. They were told it was retaliation for the Luftwaffe's destroying London and the leveling of many of the American cities, including New York. But New York stood untouched as did the cities and villages through which they passed each day. Now he made the connection with the reality that had become North Africa in the spring. As the battle wore on and the Americans joined with the British, he had seen waves of new style tanks, the sky filled with American aircraft he couldn't identify. He knew the war was lost. He fought on, but the tremendous superiority of supplies and equipment available was without end. The brilliance of Rommel was not a myth. Rommel fearless, or feeding on his own fame, was everywhere, in a front line tank, a forward bunker. Becker had thought him brilliant but also crazy or crazy brave. Now seeing this country, he knew that any invasion and battle for Europe would end as had his in North Africa. The train passed through large and small cities, neat houses everywhere, with cars parked at their homes and on the street. His wife and son had hopefully fled Dresden, while children played on the streets of the American villages he passed through. Anger and depression rode with him in tandem. In his heart, Becker knew the future for him was to wait in some Stalag until at last the war ended. His anger was manifested in his hate for Hitler and those who took his country into the war. In his alternate dream world he hoped his country could yet win and then dispose of the Nazis, restore–rebuild Germany and leave those countries to which Germany could claim no historical prerogative. In truth he knew his hopes were naïve daydreams. With occupation came greed and license and his people were not likely to go quietly from any new empire.

While still on the battlefield they had been told of a new "secret weapon" that would redefine the way a war was fought, a system that could fire deadly rockets from great distances, making bombers obsolete. There was talk of work on a bomb that in one single explosion could level a city. No such weapons were ever revealed and the soldiers came to think of the reports as an attempt to buttress the flagging morale of the battered German Army. They ignored fresh troops from the homeland who carried with them such tales.

The defeat of the elite Afrika Korps and the subsequent surrender of almost one hundred fifty thousand of its soldiers was a massive blow to the Axis powers and would be a turning point of the war.

The American train ride was a revelation. In Casablanca the prisoners had slept on the ground and were fed an issue of the British troops' rations: canned vegetables, a meat concoction, tea, and a sweet. No stoves had been provided for heating the tea, nor wood for a fire. It was not the first time Becker had eaten British rations. On more than one occasion the Afrika Korps had so swiftly overrun British positions that the Brits literally left everything but their guns and tanks. Their own supply lines tenuous at best, the Korps soldiers gladly consumed the food, as foreign as it was to them at first bite. On the train ride from New York they had been served two hot meals. Red Cross workers came on board and handed out cigarettes and shaving gear. The cars were clean, though the prisoners had to sleep sitting up or in the aisle. The accommodations were not oppressive in any way. A blanket was provided each prisoner. Unlike the wool blankets issued to the American Army, it more resembled a cover used for moving pianos but was adequate for the train travel. Was this act a prelude to what the camps would be or a cruel interlude before a severe imprisonment? Americans were a strange lot. Unexplainably positive, and even happy, Becker was wary of their care. Why would the Americans treat them well? The British, Australian, Indian, and American soldiers they had captured were not so lucky. Battlefield conditions prevented such treatment, nor was there a desire on any German soldiers' part to see comfort provided for those who fought and killed their comrades. Rommel, however, had insisted on no physical mistreatment of prisoners, and in that theater of war, his word was the last one. The Allied soldiers' stay in a German Stalag in North Africa was brief, most prisoners being sent back to Germany and East Europe for labor. Could the American POW camps be worse than North Africa with the hell-like temperatures, the sand storms, flies, the fleas? Becker remembered a proverb that says, "When Allah made Hell, He didn't find it bad enough, so he created the desert and added flies." The German soldiers developed their own versions of the Aram headdress in an attempt to counter these afflictions. The Arabs had adapted to the harsh conditions of the desert centuries ago and took great pleasure in the discomfort of both the Axis and Allied soldiers.

The sandstorms had been so severe all fighting stopped. The natives called them "ghibli." The sand clogged carburetors and made all food half grit. Vast quantities of sand could be moved by the ghibli. The natives dreaded the "evil" winds, so intense that camel masters claimed a female could become pregnant in a ghibli without the intervention of a male. The wet season began in November. The dirt roads became impassable and the tanks spent as much time pulling vehicles from the mud as they did firing at the enemy.

The Arab population was more problem than asset. They greeted each side as liberators as they alternately annexed their villages. Natives sometimes slipped into the camps in the darkness of night, or day made into night by the suffocating, blinding sandstorms. They stole supplies and slit the throats of sleeping soldiers.

Fighting alongside the Italians had been an added trial. Many of their soldiers had been brave, but their army was as disorganized as the German troops were organized and disciplined. On two occasions, Becker recalled, the Italians bombed German positions by mistake. The Italians did not really believe it was their war and sometimes fought like it. While a German soldier would never dare say a word of criticism about their Führer, the Italian troops were prone to spit when Mussolini's name was mentioned.

Otto's negative experiences with the Italians continued on the train trip to Texas. Several stops were made by the convoy of railcars. At each stop some prisoners' names were called and they were offloaded into trucks bound for camps along the route. The remaining Germans were reassigned to other cars so that all remained full. The cars that were emptied were dropped from the train. At one point, Otto traveled in a train car in which German and Italian prisoners were comingled. His distaste for his allies was further fueled by their loud behavior and their lack of civility to the Germans. Otto was told by an Italian, who spoke German, that his fellow soldiers' disrespect was a manifestation of a commonly held belief: that the Italian Army had been dragged into Germany's war. What will Italy gain from their fighting, he asked. Perhaps a part of the worthless desert or some other useless country the Germans didn't want for themselves. Italians were lovers, he said, and the only thing worth fighting over was a woman. Otto told him that the lovers shouting out the partially opened windows at every woman in the towns they passed through had brought attention to the prisoners. In one Midwest city their noise had caught the attention of a group of men who recognized their uniforms and stoned the windows of the train, showering the cars with glass. The prisoners' guards had to go out and calm the angry group, rapidly growing into mob size. The guards warned those causing a disturbance would be taken off the train and dealt with. The Italians calmed somewhat. Despite that incident, most Americans the train passed waved back at troops of both armies, either mistaking them for U.S. soldiers or simply expressing the American trait of friendliness to strangers.

Chapter 5

J.T.'S BEST FRIEND, BEU, drove him to the farm on his first day. Beu was the only kid J.T. really knew who had a car of his own, a '35 Plymouth. It was about a football field long and impossible to parallel park. Both boys had found that out when they turned fourteen and took the driver's test. Beu's dad had taught him to drive and Beu had taught J.T. They had practiced in the cemetery because Beu said, "You can't hurt anyone there," and they hadn't. Beu's full name was Beuford Mitchell Reynolds, but that mouthful became just Beu to friends and family alike. Beu was rich, at least in J.T.'s eyes. He had his own car along with an unexplained access to gas stamps which were like gold. Beu wore his hair down to his collar and didn't seem to mind what anyone thought of it. Along with being just about the smartest boy in school (with the smartest mouth, as well), the haircut made him unique. Mr. Reynolds was some sort of federal government guy who wore suits and who, and there were witnesses, had paid eleven hundred dollars cash for a new Ford in 1940, when you could still buy cars. J.T. guessed the Reynolds' house must be worth at least eight thousand dollars because he'd heard Farmer Mac say you couldn't touch it for that amount. J.T. couldn't figure out why you'd want to touch it but he'd sure pay that much to *live* there, if he could.

Beu was not driving J.T. to the farm out of the kindness of his heart or as a favor to a friend. He wanted to actually *see* a German soldier, a prisoner of war. He was curious if they would be fierce, larger-than-life warriors or resemble more their leader, Adolph Hitler. Beu had seen plenty of Hitler and Tojo pictures in the newsreels, and if their soldiers looked anything like their leaders, he figured it was all but over.

Jerome Thayer Graham had become known as J.T. for the same reason Beuford Mitchell Reynolds had become Beu. Folks known by their initials were pretty common in Texas as were boys known by both their first and middle names, like his cousin Bobby Jack. One of J.T.'s friends was Billy Ray White. All three of his names had to be used lest you mistake him for Billy Joe Menefee or Billy Don Daniels, all classmates. J.T. had been in one class with all three Billys, which had just about driven the teacher mad. Females were not immune from the two-name game. Cathy Jo, Gloria Jean, Mary Francis, and Verna Ruth all addressed as "hun" if an adult didn't know their double dipper. Juniors were in a category all their own. They were either a gift to the ego of the father or exposed a frightful shortage of imagination when the birth certificate had been thrust upon the parental couple. Junior Lumpkin was really William Marvin Lumpkin Jr. to no one except his mama. Pity even more the poor soul who was a "Little," like Little Travis Davis, not to be confused with his dad, Big Travis. Oldest sons were sometimes called *Brother* and the elder daughter, *Sister*. *Brother* sometimes took the form of *Bubba,* which on occasion had no sibling meaning but was used to describe a "good ole boy." The *Brother* and *Sister* terms of affection, or affliction, depending on your point of view, were usually confined to the household and thankfully not borne outside the family confines. It was all quite confusing to J.T. He seldom was asked to explain his initials. In Texas, they'd ask what J.T. stood for only if he were going to jail or off to war. So far, J.T. had done neither.

"Man, I can hardly wait to see some real German soldiers. Are you sure they'll be there?" asked Beu.

"Mama says they've been working on Mr. Mac's place for a while already. Now don't say anything to Farmer Mac while you're there. I don't want to lose my job before I even start it."

The Ed McConnell farm was two miles off the road that continued west to the air base and the prisoner compound. After today, J.T. would take one of the busses that ran from town to the base, get off at the McConnell road, and walk to the farm. He would return home by the same method. J.T. had pulled cotton on the McConnell farm so he was familiar with the man and his prosperous acreage. Around Warner cotton was pulled not picked. The boll was separated from the cotton at the gin and was ground into cattle feed. The seed was rendered into cottonseed oil which was used for cooking and, most exciting to J.T., in the making of explosives. As they drove to the farm, J.T. could see that Mr. Mac's cotton was already up. He figured he would be out in those fields chopping cotton soon, ridding it of weeds that sucked at its growth. J.T. didn't mind, he'd done it before. He liked to work, which was a necessity for his family and not really a hardship for a fifteen-year-old boy with boundless energy.

"Old Mac will work you till your balls drop off, J.T. Ya know that? He's a real shit."

"Oh, he's okay, Beu. I've worked here before."

"Well, he's a cretin in my opinion."

Cretin was Beu's latest word. He got it from Miss Daniels' "Word of the Day" in their freshman English class and used it as noun, adjective, and a substitute for any word needed to complete a sentence. *Habitual* had been *cretin's* predecessor, but it was a goner once Beu found he could call people an idiot and receive only a blank look, not a fist.

A field of grain sorghum replaced the rows of cotton as they neared the farmhouse. Ed McConnell's father had once been wiped out by the boll weevil and he had learned to vary and rotate his crops. He had planted wind rows, or shelter belts, long before they became widely used, thus the McConnell farm had survived the Dust Bowl as few others had. Trees were prominent on the McConnell place, shin oak, salt cedar, cottonwood, and pecan among them. Then there were the useless mesquite, treated more like a weed since no one could think of any reason to preserve them.

Beu pulled into the farmyard and parked near the barn. Ed McConnell walked out to meet them. He was a tall, thin man with a leathery face and enormous hands.

"Howdy, J.T."

"Howdy, Mr. Mac. You know my friend, Beu, don't you?"

"Yeah, I remember Beu. I just need one hand, Beuford, if you came looking for a job."

"No, sir, I'm not lookin' to work. I just gave J.T. a ride. Where're the Germans?"

"They're working, just like everybody else. All right, J.T. I got a form for you to fill out for the gov'ment. Required since you'll be working around the prisoners. Like I told you, the pay is $1.25 a day, most Saturdays and Sundays off. I pay the government a dollar a day for each prisoner. They get eighty cents of it back at the base they can use for cigarettes and the like. Ain't no officers or NCOs here. They don't work. Gov'ment gives them three dollars a month for just sitting on their ass back at the camp You got house and outhouse privileges, the prisoners have a shovel to bury their droppin's. Your main job will be the pigs. You'll be working in the fields once you feed them and haul off their shit. Sound good so far, son?" Mac grinned.

"Sounds cretin to me," Beu muttered.

"What's that?" Mr. Mac fairly shouted.

"Sounds creative to me, sir."

"Now about the Krauts, J.T."

"I never thought I'd be around anyone who fought in a war," said J.T.

"Those Krauts ain't heroes, boy. They're prisoners and just awhile ago they were killing our boys. Don't ever forget that. They *are* the enemy. They're pretty tame right now. Only got one guard here with 'em, but don't get too relaxed 'cause of that. They're the enemy sho'nuff."

"You told me you could drive. Is that right?"

"Oh, yesser."

"Well, every other day you'll go into the base with the truck and haul back a couple of barrels of slop for the pigs. Can you do that?"

"Yes sir!"

"First thing I want you to do is go meet the prison guard that stays with these Germans every day."

"How many Germans?"

"Ten to fifteen, depending on the work. Now, you see that soldier leaning against the tree down in the south field?"

"Yes sir."

"Go down there and meet him so'ans he knows you belong on the place, ya hear?"

J.T. headed for the field and Beu began with him.

"Beuford, you go down and have a look at *real* Germans and then you come back up here and git. J.T.'s going to work and you're leavin'."

Both boys mouthed *Yes sir* at the same time and hurriedly left to have their first up-close look at the enemy.

They approached the soldier, who didn't move from the shade. He had watched them closely as they approached. He had a rifle slung over his shoulder and a pistol belt holding a .45. Blue-clad prisoners worked nearby. On one leg of their pants was a "P," the other a "W," and "POW" was stenciled in large letters on the backs of their shirts.

"Howdy sir, my name's J.T. and this my friend Beu. I'll be working on the farm and Beu won't."

"So it's J.T. and Beu, huh. Sorry to hear your barber died, Beu."

"What?"

"Well, gentlemen, I'm Sergeant William Preston, United States Military Police."

"Holy shit," said Beu. *"Sergeant Preston of the Yukon!"*

"That's one of my favorite radio programs," said J.T., "'On, you huskies! On!' Listen to it every week."

"I bet you do," said Preston. "Probably listen to *Let's Pretend* and *Peter Rabbit's Playhouse,* too, don't you?"

"No sir, not really. My mama likes Bob Hope 'cause she thinks maybe he's visiting someplace where my brother's fighting."

"Well, we know one thing for sure. Bob Hope's ain't gonna put on a show at Branch Camp 67, is he?"

A tall POW stepped forward.

"And you are the worker sent to make our life easier. Is that right, mein Freund?"

"You speak English?" said a wide-eyed J.T.

"Yes, a bit. My name is Otto Becker."

"Glad to meet you, sir."

"You don't call me sir. I'm a German prisoner."

"My mama says I should call everybody *Sir* who's an adult, sir."

"Your mama is wrong. What is your name?"

"J.T., sir."

"J.T.? That's not a name, those are two letters of the alphabet."

"Jerome Thayer, sir, that's what the J.T. stands for."

"I think I shall just call you mein Freund."

"What does that mean?"

"My friend, but then we can't really be friends, can we, Jerome? A German prisoner of war cannot be your friend. Maybe, work friend? You see, I can't call someone by letters. My friends don't call me O.F. Becker, that would make them laugh. And it sounds like an insulting word in your language. Oaf Becker, ridiculous. I'm already called Crazy Otto. That is enough for one man."

"Crazy Otto?" said J.T.

Otto ignored him. "What would be better than mein Freund for this strong young man who has come to ease our workload?"

"All right, Becker," said Sergeant Preston, "No one cares what you call the kid."

"I don't mind mein Freund, sir."

"Oh, repeated with the German accent as well. Are you German?"

"No sir, I'm Texan."

"Are there German people in your family? You would pass very well in my country, blond hair, blue eyes. They would think you the perfect Aryan, the pure one. Families would welcome you into their homes, touch your hair, look with admiration into your blue eyes. We impure only take the scraps from your genetic banquet."

"I don't understand a word you're saying."

"Never mind, Jerome. I think I will just call you Kumpel for now, maybe friends someday."

"What's a kumpel?"

"Like your word *buddy*. You will be Kumpel, my buddy. Now I get back to work, Kleiner Kumpel. I see the farmer looking at us. We will talk another time."

Chapter 6

THE HOUSE WHERE J.T., his mother, and grandmother lived was a two-story relic of the early century that had Victorian ambitions but had settled for less. The landlady, who occupied the other half of the downstairs and all the upstairs rooms, was a church lady friend of Mama's who had made room for them when they could no longer afford the small house that J.T. had called home for five years. His brother and sister had contributed to the rent then, but once they left, Mama had only what she could bring in ironing clothes and washing dishes at local cafés. Grandma's small pension barely covered the discarded and purchased hearing aids that arrived almost monthly. Grandma had become Alma Graham's burden, and expense, by the simple fact that Alma was a widow. She had three sisters but she had drawn the short straw when their father passed away. Actually, no drawing had taken place. Since Mama was the only one without a husband, Grandma moving in with Alma seemed to be a logical choice, *to them*. "The company will be nice for you, Alma." "Burton and Mama never got along, Alma. You know that. She wouldn't be happy with us." "Mama wouldn't want to live way down in Houston, so far away from her friends and church." Alma didn't argue the case. She knew that all three husbands wanted nothing to do with housing a brittle, opinionated old lady who mutually detested them.

Thad, aka PFC Thadius Louis Graham, USMC, had directed all his pay, combat allowance included, to be sent to Mama each month. She, in turn, banked every cent in a savings account for him. Alma now worked in the Officers Mess at the air base, helping prepare the food, then serving it to the men as they filed past with their plates and trays. The air base job had been a step up for Alma Graham. The pay was better and medical treatment was available for her family. J.T. was a healthy teen and Grandma was on the way to living a century, deaf but acquiescent to few of the frailties common to eighty-five-year-olds. Only Alma had needed help.

In the front window of the Graham apartment hung a small service flag, or Blue Star Banner as some called it. It was a shiny, silk-like cloth with a white background, red border, and blue stars. Each of the two stars represented a member of the household serving in the armed forces. J.T.'s sister Susan, the youngest daughter, was a WAAC stationed at Fort Sill, Oklahoma. Three other sisters were married and had children of their own. If either Susan or Thad had gotten leave and visited, it would have been a tight fit indeed. The duplex was a three-room accommodation consisting of a living room, bedroom, and tiny kitchen. Mama slept with Grandma in the only bed while J.T. occupied the couch with bad springs. The couch did not fold down and its pillows smelled of age or some encounter with a spilled liquid. A stain remained like a round target in the center cushion. J.T. slept on his right side or back most of the night to avoid turning his face into the aroma. At least once a night he sucked in its essence and tried to hold it in his nose and mouth as a part of his determination to identify his nightly bed partner. Mama said it was just "stale," but J.T. didn't know what stale was supposed to smell like. He had asked Beu if he'd come over sometime for a guest smell but he had declined, declaring that J.T.'s stink, when he picked him up from a day with hogs, was plenty enough for him. J.T. studied at the small kitchen table or on the couch if Grandma did not have her quilting frame up. Other than reading the Bible and ordering hearing aids, quilting occupied her day. She did excellent work, or so people said. The quilts were colorful, the blocks made from discarded material of all sorts: dresses, chicken feed and flour sacks, scarves, colorful scraps of all sorts or from other quilts past their prime, fit only for cannibalization or use as dishrags or towels. Grandma took cotton, straight from the fields, and combed the seeds from it with two metal combs. The blocks were separated by a one-color material she called sashing, which she sewed together on her pedal-driven sewing machine and affixed to the edges of the quilts as well as the separated blocks. She made heavy quilts and "summer" quilts by the adding or deleting of cloth and cotton. She had made a quilt for every grandchild, embroidered with their name in the middle. J.T. had slept in the familiar warmth of his since he could remember. It was the only item he was sure he would take should he decide to set out for adventures Warner, Texas, could not offer.

The Sunday afternoon was quiet except for an occasional outburst from a woodpecker assaulting the pecan tree outside their window. J.T. was reading a book but mostly studying his mother, who earlier had dabbed tears from her eyes as she stated, to no one in particular, "It's been two months since we got a letter." J.T. hadn't answered and Grandma likely hadn't heard. It was the second time she had silently cried that day. At church that morning the preacher had said a prayer for all the boys and girls called off to war. Mama had gripped his hand during the prayer, then released it to search out a handkerchief in her purse.

J.T. looked at her legs, wrapped in cloth with a metal fastener. The years of standing labor had created varicose veins that required surgery. To J.T. the wrapping was mummy-like and reminded him of the movie *The Invisible Man,* one of his favorites. *The Invisible Man* only took on human form when his invisible body was wrapped, then dressed in a suit topped by a fashionable fedora. Don the clothes and hat, unwrap the mummy stuff, and there was nobody there. Being invisible was one of J.T.'s favorite fantasies. Would Mama's legs disappear when the wrapping was removed? If so, she might be able to join J.T., the invisible teenager, as he fought crime and harassed Beu into one of his cursing tirades. But J.T. knew how Mama's exposed legs looked, and they would not be invisible. Blue, raised veins ran over them like a road map. Dark blue highways, with lighter country roads that ran parallel and then crossed at random points. Those were the hard features of calves once strong and handsome. J.T. was by nature a positive and optimistic person, happy to a fault some said, but the sight of Mama's legs left him low down and sad. He felt guilty for being such a chicken liver but when Mama took off her wrappings, J.T. looked away.

"What does Mr. McConnell have you doing now, J.T.?"

"Same stuff, Mama. I mainly tend the hogs and work with the prisoners in the fields or chore stuff like feeding the chickens. You know, farm stuff. Mucking the pens is the worst part. He lets me drive the truck, ya know."

"Lord, the man's lost his mind."

"I drive into the base every other day and pick up the slop barrels from the two mess halls and bring it back."

"How does a boy like you load and unload a barrel full of slop?"

"The prisoners help me—on both ends."

Mama returned to writing her letter.

"Who you writing, Mama?"

"Your Aunt Florence."

"You write a lot of letters, Mama."

"I love to *get* letters. And how do you get letters, J.T.?"

"You write'um, Mama."

"Yes, you do."

"You need some more pants, J.T. When you get paid."

"Get him overalls, Alma," Grandma chimed in from nowhere.

"I don't want to wear overalls, Grandma. Beu says they look cretin."

"Your grandpa wore them every day of his life."

"Yeah, but that was back in the Stone Age, Grandma. This is 1944."

"Don't argue with your grandma, and go in and lay out your work gloves with your clothes and hat." Mama went back to her letter and Grandma to the Bible, and no one seemed to care about continuing the dialogue.

"Mama?"

"Yes."

"I need a girlfriend."

"You don't need any such thing."

"Well everybody keeps asking me, 'Do yew got a girlfriend, J.T.?' 'Were yew late 'cause you were with your girlfriend last night?'"

"Humph," said Mama.

"Everybody but Mr. Mac says I need a girlfriend."

"Well he'd say that."

"He says if it has tits or a transmission it's gonna cause you trouble someday."

"J.T.! I don't want to hear that word from your mouth again."

"What word?"

"Your word for breasts, that's what!"

"Is that a bad word? That's what they call a cow's …"

"That's teats," Mama interrupted. "It's not the same."

"Do the same job, don't they?"

"Enough, J.T.!"

"Why'd you say Mr. McConnell *would* say I shouldn't get a girl?"

"Never you mind. Mr. Mac is your employer. His business is none of yours. You're a farm hand and you are not to ever ask him anything personal. Put your work gloves out now like I told you and go in and throw away those crawdads. You know I told ya'll they come from that lake full of oil the compress dumps in there and they're not fit to eat.

"Beu eats them."

"There you go, another good reason to *not* eat them right there. And one more thing, young man, before you get up. You stay away from those prisoners, you hear?"

"Mama, I work with them every day. They're good fellers."

"They're the *enemy*, J.T. They killed our boys before they came here. They're dangerous."

"Aw, Mama, they're glad they are prisoners. They don't want any more trouble. They only have one guard. If they wanted to hurt him or run away, it would be easy."

"Gloves, crawdads, and mind what I say about those men."

"Yes, ma'am."

Chapter 7

LOCATING THE AIR BASE at Warner had been a financial blessing and a bragging point the several towns of a similar size within a thirty-mile radius could not claim. The base had been constructed with some local labor and materials. Once constructed, the off-duty airmen and the married officers who lived in town gave new life to retail and housing. Add the bonus of on-base civilian jobs, the cheap farm labor provided by the prisoners, and Warner prospered as never before. Prisoners of War, of course, were a great source of interest and curiosity. The reaction to the attention paid them by the civilian population was mixed. Most of the soldiers waved back to those who acknowledged them thusly, and of course, pretty girls received the prisoners' best grins, waves, and comments, thankfully not translated. Other POWs became surly upon civilian recognition, commenting that they have come to see us like animals in a zoo.

It was not uncommon to have a car pull to the side of the road to observe the men in the fields or working alongside the highway removing debris. Prisoners were also observed in passing trucks, occasionally unloading materials from freight cars, and new prisoners were sometimes met and quickly removed from incoming trains. But as far as anyone could discern, Private Otto Becker was the first to pay an individual, unaccompanied, visit to town.

Chapter 8

COLONEL PAYNE SHUFFLED THROUGH papers that awaited his signature, watching the clock, girding himself for a task he had avoided since he took command, a question-and-answer session the mayor of Warner had presumptuously labeled "a meeting of the minds." And at what point of understanding war does a civilian mind *meet* a military one? If form held, the mayor would not have a clue. He'd never met the man, but he was sure that's how it would go. The man had given his attitude away with the "meeting of the minds" crap, hadn't he? At least Mr. Mayor hadn't blindsided him. Early on, he had shared some of his "concerns" in a rambling letter and had closed with a request that a "confab" be arranged. In the letter, the mayor had revealed his day job to be that of a pharmacist. He didn't say if he'd ever been in the military or how he was avoiding it now.

The sergeant typist who manned the Base Commander's outer office tapped lightly on the door and stuck his head in. "The mayor's here, sir."

"Show him in," said Colonel Payne, rising and moving in front of the desk to meet his fellow "mind." The mayor was a professorial-looking fellow, painfully thin, round glasses too large for his face, and a hairline that had receded halfway back on his head, the thin, remaining strands clipped closely on the sides and top. His voice belied his look, being deep in register and seemingly pushed up to his mouth by an active Adam's apple.

The mayor extended his hand and spoke first. "Lloyd Kimbel, Colonel. It's good to meet you in person."

"Thanks for driving out, Mr. Mayor. Have a seat. Cigarette?" the colonel asked, offering a package of Camels.

"No, thank you. Got my own. They say Camel smokers drive Chevys. Is that right?"

"Well, I drive the Jeep line, natural air-conditioning model, myself. And the car back in Illinois is an Oldsmobile."

"Then I was misinformed."

"How can I help you, sir? I assume you'd like to discuss the things you mentioned in your letter?"

"First, I'd like you to understand I'm reflecting the thoughts of the good citizens of Warner, and I may or may not agree with them."

"Fair enough. I represent the United States Army Air Force and the U.S. Government, and I don't always agree with them, either."

"I'll just kind of go down the questions, then, take some notes if you don't mind, uh, like I was a reporter for *Life* or *Collier's* or something." Colonel Payne did not answer.

The mayor cleared his throat and started. "The biggest complaint I get, every time someone brings up the prisoners, is how well they're being treated. Treated better than the folks in Warner. Three big meals a day, bacon, sausage, and butter. Butter! That's the one that gets the ladies. We can't *get* butter, Colonel. You ever see one of the ladies mix that margarine? Take that gooey bunch of lard-looking stuff and work the color package contents into the gook to make the color of butter. And here's men who fought and killed our boys eatin' better than us. Folks are calling your *prison* the Fritz Ritz and the Wolfgang Waldorf and the such. Gabriel Heatter and Walter Winchell talk about it on their radio programs. Drew Pearson writes about it, and it makes people mad. The folks cook up the Spam and beans, then they see the POWs out in the fields, well-fed and just doin' fine. Damn sight better than they were doing when they were losing battles and being taken prisoner. Ed McConnell picks up the leavin's from your prisoner mess hall and he says they throw away more than some people got. I have a cousin in Florida who sent me an article from the *Tampa Tribune*. Here it is, says, 'The Germans Shoot Their Prisoners:

We Feed Them Shortcake.' People are probably upset wherever there's a POW camp."

"Makes me just as angry as it does the civilians, Mr. Mayor. I don't like it a damn bit."

"Well, why you doing it, then?"

"You ever heard of the Geneva Convention, Mayor? Agreed upon and signed in 1929. It's the rules for war. Among those rules is how prisoners are to be treated. We signed it, so did Germany. Japan, Russia, and some others did not."

"I've heard of it."

"Covers about everything concerning prisoners of war, medical care, torture, living quarters, mail. They pretty much get it all, have it all in writing. As for food, it is a little more vague than other parts, says they must be kept in good health, fed in a manner to promote that. What's happened is the Red Cross, Swiss people, those who have appointed themselves protectors of these men, have interpreted the feeding part to say the prisoners must be served rations of the same quality as their captors. So long and short of it, they pretty much eat what we eat. One of their men was a chef so he does their cooking, so not only do they eat well, they have some of the dishes native to Germany."

"That's outrageous! Put them all in Death Valley and let them starve to death, for my money."

"Yeah, well that's not going to happen, Mayor. I fed them bread and water for two days when they acted up. Got hell for that. Your beef, pardon the pun, is with the Allied High Command and the Department of War."

"They don't think the Germans are treating our boys the same way, do they?"

"Actually, that's one of the reasons they give as to why they must be treated this way. They believe that if the word gets back to Germany that we are behaving humanely toward their men, then our boys who are captured will be imprisoned in a like manner."

"Bacon and butter and get paid to work?"

"Wouldn't think so. Eisenhower believes in the strategy, though. He's ordered flyers to be dropped behind German lines telling them if they surrender they'll be given all the perks we're talking about."

"Is it working?"

"Too early to tell, they say. All right, I hear their bitch on the Fritz Ritz, now what else?"

"Do your men have to salute the Nazi officers?"

"Course not."

"And do the Nazis use the Nazi salute?"

"Not to my men, but they're allowed to use it inside the compound only with each other. One of the things that has made my life easier is that they discipline themselves in their living area very well. Sometimes the discipline becomes a little rough, but that's okay by me long as it's not killing rough. You see, Mayor, I was *not* trained to be a warden. I hate this new job they've given me. I'm a pilot and a bombardier. I was in the 8th Air Force, first battles we got into. I was wounded and I wound up here teaching other people how to bomb the enemy. So getting back to the subject, I don't care if they use their damned Nazi salute, don't really care if they live or die, but I have my duty, my job." The colonel's phone rang. The colonel listened, then said, "He wants what? Hell no, I won't. Bring von Hoffmann to my office in an hour. First go over and bring me a record player and something so country your neck turns red just listening to it. Can you do that? Very well."

"Sorry about that, Mayor. It's my beady-eyed little SS officer with another demand, wants their own music this time."

"People are worried about prisoners escaping, Colonel. One man did come into town."

"I don't think you could label that an escape. We call that guy Crazy Otto, a whole 'nother story, Otto is. No, there have been several escapes from POW camps around the country. We get the reports. There has not been one case in which one of the escapees hurt a civilian, committed a violent crime or sabotage. They know that they would be hung before the week was out. West Texas is not a place you'd want to escape in any way. We're a long way from Germany, Mr. Mayor. No, I have that SS officer who gives me more to think about than prisoners escaping. His BS and my airmen going into your town on their time off."

"Your men have behaved themselves for the most part, Colonel. Our girls sure like having all the young males around, especially since most of ours are gone." The mayor checked off "escape danger" and moved down his list.

"Some of the folks have complained about the noise of your bombs. Irma Shoemaker is the one who complains most at our town meetings, says her chickens are scared by the noise, not laying eggs like they used to, cows not givin' as much milk ..."

"Has Miss Shoemaker's house ever been bombed?"

"Why no, I don't ..."

"You tell her the next time we scare her chickens to ask herself how she'd feel if she were an English lady who goes down into a bomb shelter, comes out and her house has been leveled by German bombs or rockets and not only do the chickens not lay, they don't *exist!*"

"I'll do that." The mayor paused as if picturing Irma Shoemaker's farm after a bomb attack. "But is it necessary to bomb our lake? That's some of our drinking water, Colonel."

"That's what we call skip bombing, Mayor. The boys are learning how to skip a bomb across water and hit a ship. Let me be clear, Mayor. We are—at—*war.* The colonel's chin jutted out and his voice rose. These boys here will soon go to a theater of war. They'll get in their planes and risk their lives over enemy territory, dropping bombs, skipping bombs. Some of them won't come back. Never see their homes and families again! If we scare the cows and dogs, spay the chickens, stampede the cattle, it's just too damn bad. If we don't fight the enemy with everything we have, someday these prisoners you see here doing your stoop labor will be occupying our country, your town. They'll eat those animals and have their way with your women. That's harsh, but those are the facts."

"I didn't mean to anger you, Colonel." The mayor's voice was firm. He was not intimidated. "I realize I'm all hat and no cattle here, you're wearing the eagles, but I have my job to do and you have yours."

The colonel lit another Camel and exhaled with a sigh.

"Yes we do, Mayor. We have a job to do, is right. So now you know our position here. If I could address all your concerns, I would. My anger wasn't directed at you. You're not the enemy. I have three hundred and fifty of them here and your people need to know I don't operate a vacation resort on purpose. This is all new to me, trial-and-error learning. It's been hard the last few months, no fault of yours.

"Didn't take it that way at all, Colonel. I'm pretty thick-skinned, and thick-headed too, unfortunately. I sympathize with all you have on your plate.

"That's just about all I need to cover today, sir." The mayor rose to leave. "Maybe we can do this again, soon," he said.

The colonel winced at the thought and showed the mayor to the door.

The mayor paused before leaving. "Oh, and the answer to the question you wanted to ask, I have flat feet."

Chapter 9

THE PRISONERS OF CAMP 67 came from all stations of life, many religions (except Jewish), from the educated to the illiterate, the accomplished and the common man, teenage to four decades, the brave, the cowards, and the survivors. As with the mayor, food was one topic of conversation they could all share. Meals were the three highlights of their constricted day, part of a narrow focus that got them through the hours. They hadn't eaten this well in recent memory. Their country's depression shortages had been followed by the ascension of Nazi Germany. Food began to be siphoned from the people's markets to feeding a military that became more unbounded with each passing year. The home front had not improved with the early German invasion successes. Otto's wife, before the letters stopped, had told of the worsening food situation in Dresden saying meat was a luxury to be found only on the black market.

Breakfast that morning had been bread, butter, eggs, bacon, sausage, and coffee or milk. A lunch was packed for all workers, on and off base, consisting of a sandwich, fruit, carrots, and a cookie. Otto thought the American fools for feeding them this way. He knew the Allied prisoners would not be fed as well, nor would German troops or civilians. *How can we be losing a war to such a soft people?*

It was dinnertime now, a respite to which Otto looked forward, not only for the food but also the opportunity to talk to his friend Hans, the "koch." Otto and Hans had been together in the Afrika Korps, surviving a lost division only to be joined in a new one. Hans lived in the NCO/

officers barracks as per Geneva Convention directive. He chose not to follow another one of its tenets that said Sergeant Hans Schroeder did not have to work. Hans, you see, *was the chef,* and in this monotonous confinement likely its most popular, if not most powerful, resident. Hans had taken over the kitchen shortly after his arrival in the camp. He had been unable to stand either his own idleness or the sludgy swill turned out by the inexperienced soldiers assigned to food preparation. His first project had been to convince the Americans that their white bread was an insult to civilized cuisine. Hans had been given most of the ingredients to create four loaves, two of German black bread and two of forest rye. The products of his first baking were enjoyed by the base officers, who gave permission to bake it daily for the prisoners, *if,* he would teach the base baker the skill. Hans did so, even including his "secret" method of spraying the oven with water to enhance the crust. The German bread became a favorite with the airmen, though a number continued to eat Wonder bread, preferring it for its "neutral versatility."

Two of Otto's closest friends at Camp 67, Hans and Klaus Lang, spoke English as did he. Klaus worked in the bombing zones, setting up targets and locating unexploded bombs that had buried themselves. Otto had told Klaus that he didn't have to do that dangerous work and was crazier than Crazy Otto for doing so, but Klaus enjoyed the freedom of the job, as well as the danger.

The three talked daily of trivial matters, sometimes momentous matters in a trivial way, cognizant, as they were, of their inability to influence either.

The three men took great pleasure in needling each other at dinnertime, safe, they believed, in an assumption that the other soldiers didn't understand the English and didn't care if they did. Some may have enjoyed the two privates giving as good as they got in a taunting exchange with a sergeant.

"Good evening, Sergeant Schroeder!" said Otto, arms outstretched as if expecting an embrace. "How is the Metzger of fine dining?"

"Ah, if it isn't my friend Crazy Otto, the Dresden Dummkopf. How are things in the village? The beer, the women? Waiting for your return? And who is this with you? Private Sour Kraut, the bomb digger? Still in one piece—amazing!"

"You are the only place open, Herr Schroeder, so *once* again ..." Klaus let his dramatically weary voice trail off.

"Gentlemen, tonight you have come to the right place. I am happy my many competitors are not open, because I have for you sauerbraten like fit for the Führer's table itself. Beef from the cows Farmer Otto tends, marinated overnight in spicy vinegar water mit my secret herbs added and served with red cabbage and potato dumplings."

"That's all and fine, sir," said Otto. "But I don't see any German sausage. I ask you once again, *when* do we get German sausage?"

"Patience, patience, my friend, the wurst is yet to come." The routine was a familiar one that sent them into gales of laughter while the other prisoners sat stone-faced and puzzled.

After they finished their meal, Hans came to the table where Otto and Klaus sat alone.

"Fine sauerbraten, my friend," said Otto.

"Ja, ja, not bad for Club 67," said Klaus.

"Just remember, gentlemen, the food before I began cooking."

"You're right. I shut up," Klaus snapped.

"So what news, Hans?"

"We are getting mail now, as you know."

"Not me," Otto interrupted.

"Regardless, some are. Zimmerman got a letter that said his brother had been killed at Normandy."

"Sorry to hear that," said Otto. "The war cuts both ways, as we well know. Zimmerman can grieve, but he must remember in his two years in the Korps he sent bad news to many mothers as well. That is war."

"War, war, war. We're not fighting a war, we're just hearing about it, reading about it. Look at us, Otto, Klaus. Three men, educated with careers. How did we come to this? Did we do the right thing?"

"You are really asking if Germany did the right thing, Hans. It's a waste of time to address questions that are time passed and beyond our power to influence. We have been reduced to the lowest form of German existence. I find blame, but it is useless to dwell on. And remember, it is not for us to say we did the right thing. We were told to serve our country's effort, and we did. We did." Otto was again the teacher, answering the unanswerable questions.

"We may be here for years."

"Do you really think it will take that long, Hans?"

"Careful, Otto, those are treasonous words. We still don't know who is a hardcore Nazi and who is not."

"And what would von Hoffmann and his *schlägers* do if they heard us, Hans, put us on report, court martial us, demote us? We're privates already."

Hans bent closer and spoke softly to the two men. "Don't take it lightly, Otto. Just yesterday von Hoffmann punched Richter in the face because he spoke favorably of the treatment he had received from a guard. Then he proceeded to berate him for ten minutes and slapped him again."

"And Richter did nothing? He's a lieutenant as well, Hans. Why should he not fight back?"

"It's the SS, Otto, obviously. Everyone is afraid. We were trained that way. You know that. He uses other methods, some you've seen, I'm sure, notes left on bunks, threats that he has connections in Germany who would harm our families."

"So he'd just ring up Berlin and give that order. Do you believe that?"

"There's the mail, Otto. He writes a lot of letters, for our benefit to see. He's leaked the word he has a code to communicate information to the High Command."

"'Bullshit!' as Sergeant Preston would say."

"Perhaps, but now there is the radio. I believe they have rigged for shortwave. The next step would be they make it a transmitter."

"We can't live in fear of that *Schweinehund*. It's hard enough without that. We work in the fields all day and he sits on his scrawny little ass. You can bet some officers wrote that part of the Geneva Convention. The SS in charge in Texas, behind barbed wire, no guns, no tanks, just a little man slapping his gloves to his hand? Let me tell you something, my friends. I think von Hoffmann is a phony and maybe even more."

"You think he is not SS?" asked Klaus.

"He has shown us the tattoo under his left arm, Otto," said Hans. "It looks authentic."

"Oh, he's SS all right. It's just that he's commanding us, 'Do this, say that, don't do that.' We fight the war for four years, some here longer. He never fought, never saw combat."

"But he was captured in North Africa like us," Hans said. "How could that be?"

"Ask Private Fuchs, if he will talk to you. He was an orderly at the command post just before the Kasserine Pass. He said von Hoffmann and another SS officer arrived there and stayed two days. He doesn't think they ever talked with Rommel, but officers in the command clearly did not like them, or perhaps their mission. Sometimes SS were sent to discipline officers or remove them from command. Fuchs doesn't know what they did at Kasserine, but he observed they were pompous asses who walked into a front line battalion like they were in charge. Then later, the battalion officers found out that the two had not come from a fighting unit at all. They had seen no action, no combat, because they were part of the operation of Jewish work camps! He doesn't know what that had to do with coming to North Africa, but there was speculation that the camps were not work camps."

"What, if no work?" asked Klaus.

"Extermination, I think," said Otto. "I had heard those rumors before, when new troops joined our units. They said things like, 'The Russian Front is good, and the Jewish Front is even better,' and laugh. Then I took it to mean Jews were still being rounded up. My wife had told me that in letters."

"Dangerous," said Hans.

"Yes. I wrote her not to mention it again."

"So Fuchs doesn't know what von Hoffmann's mission was, then. Maybe just a message boy from the High Command in Berlin?"

"Fuchs says no officer was removed. It was no time for social visits, either. Kasserine was just days away, so …"

"And that's not the end of the story. Apparently von Hoffmann was taken prisoner on the way back to where they were to be picked up by air transportation. His partner was killed. I'd say that one incident was the total war experience of the heroic Werner von Hoffmann."

"And now he strikes fear in our hearts and we lower our voices when we mention his name?" Otto said with disgust. Hans clearly did not want to discuss von Hoffmann further. Otto understood. Hans had daily contact with the SS officer, slept a few feet away, and Otto was sure he heard even more than he shared.

"I confess I never heard of the labor camps for the Jews being anything else but labor, Otto. Are there many?"

"I don't know, Hans. I have heard names. Dachau, I know the area, but Auschwitz and Treblinka, I have no idea. Not in Germany, I think. There may be many more. This is all I've heard."

"A camp like that would need several von Hoffmanns, I think."

"We may be getting into something we should not pursue, men. I am a chef, not a detective. Also, perhaps we should not continue our frivolity so loudly and regularly. We need to sort out the hardcore and come to know who they are and how far they would go to be in control of the camp. One more thing you should be aware. He is talking escape with some of the other officers. How, when, how many I don't know, but I think he is serious."

"Well, I'm sure he won't invite me along since our discussion earlier. Not that I would join *him,* even if we walked out the gate into a waiting plane with dancing girls and champagne."

"In that case, I'd take your spot, Otto," laughed Klaus.

Several officers and NCOs entered the mess hall and looked over at the two privates.

"Ja, meine Freunde, feeding time for the sharks. You must leave now," Hans whispered.

Otto and Klaus walked to the door as von Hoffmann entered. Von Hoffmann curled his lip in his favorite sneer. Neither Otto nor Klaus saluted.

Chapter 10

FRIDAY NIGHTS IN SMALL-TOWN Texas, when football's not in season, could test teenage creativity. Tonight, J.T. and Beu had dragged Main several times in Beu's car, then retired to Kimbel's Drug Store for a cherry Coke at the soda fountain. They had tried waving at cars with girls inside and had created some interest from afar. When the girls had pulled alongside at the railroad tracks, where the loop ends, they had looked at the two boys with an expression that would surely require an antacid. Now Kimbel's seemed a better choice than abject rejection.

Both boys were leafing through magazines from the rack just inside the front door, a forbidden practice when Mr. Kimbel was present but tonight Walter Avery, the night soda clerk, was too involved in a conversation with three girls to look or care.

"Beu, look at this Charles Atlas ad. Soon as I save enough money, I'm a fixin' to get that course and make Dynamic-Tension my life."

"You've said that about four thousand times. I should just give you the money for the thing so's you'd shut up about it."

"Look here, Beu, he's just a skinny guy like us and this bully kicks sand in his face. Then he goes out and gets the Charles Atlas course …"

"Yeah, I see. He comes back and punches the guy's lights out. Simple as that."

"J.T., I know a guy that got this course. All he does is push one fist into the other palm and keeps doing it real hard, then switches up. Just pushing against your own resistance. And you want to pay almost five dollars for that?"

"Beu, you know there's got to be more to it than that. Probably equipment and such. You don't come back to the beach looking like this guy by just pushing one fist against the other."

"Have it your way then, Tarzan," said Beu, going back to his *National Geographic* still hoping this was an issue with those native gals going naked.

The boys saw Eddie Jackson and Poot Meyer enter but figured they were headed to where the girls sat chatting with Walter Avery. Instead, they stopped and spoke. This was unusual in itself. Eddie Jackson was the star quarterback, big man on campus taken to the tenth power. Poot was on the team too, but neither boy could remember his position. At school, their attitude toward freshmen had been as Farmer Mac's saying went, "cold enough to freeze the balls off a pool table." But Eddie spoke.

"Hey, how you fellers doin'?"

"Uh, fine, I guess," said J.T. warily, expecting a putdown to follow.

"We just saw you as we walked by and came in to find out if you'd been out to visit Irene."

"Irene who?" said Beu.

"I can't give you her last name. Only a couple of us know it."

"Is she a senior?"

"No, she don't go to school. 'Bout ten years past that. Look, can I trust y'all not to blab it all over town if I tell you?" The boys hesitated.

"Aw shoot, I shouldn't bother you two cowboys. You're probably meeting some girls later."

"No, no," said J.T. quickly.

"Yeah, not till later," Beu added.

"Well, now keep this under your hat like I said. You see, Irene is this beautiful wife of a farmer nearby. She lives on this farm, but they mainly run cattle and horses. Irene's husband goes up to Fort Worth once ever couple of months to buy calves at the stockyard. He sometimes stays a week, and when he's gone ... not sure how to say this." Eddie paused, looking right and left to be sure no one overheard the privileged information he was sharing. "You see, when he's gone, Irene gets kinda lonely."

"Doesn't she have any kids or folks out there?" J.T. asked.

"No, nobody. Just her and her husband. She don't handle being alone very well."

Beu summoned up his courage and added a nonchalant tone. "What does that have to do with us?"

"Oh, a lot. You're Beuford, right?"

"Beu."

"You see, Beu, she's lonely and she likes the company of young fellers. Even younger than me and Poot, unfortunately."

"The *company* of?"

"Hey, I don't have to spell it out for you, do I? You're two good-lookin' boys. I'm sure you've been in *the company* of lots of girls before. And you're just the age Irene likes."

"Okay, Eddie, what's the joke?" Beu smiled an unsure smile, but closed his *National Geographic*.

"No joke, boys. Irene's an acquaintance of mine and I told her I'd look around and see about someone that fits her needs."

"Needs?"

"'Needs,' that's how Irene puts it. 'A lady's got her needs.'"

"If you want, Poot and me could take you out to her place and you could talk to her. Maybe she could tell you what she's missin', you know what I mean?"

"You're about fifteen, right?"

"Almost sixteen," Beu fibbed.

"Pistol-perfect age, boys! Man, this gets better all the time."

"What'd we talk about?" asked J.T.

"I don't know," said Poot. "Just talk. Fill up her lonely night, but I 'spect more. She'd probably make that all pretty clear right off, I'd bet." Poot grinned and shook his head up and down slowly.

"So, you boys in?" said Eddie, matching Poot's leering grin.

"I guess so."

"Great. We'll pick you up in front of Woolworth's in an hour. You are two *lucky* boys. You have to promise you'll tell us all the details after. Deal?"

"Deal," said the boys in unison.

Eddie and Poot arrived on time. They motioned the boys into the back seat. Eddie ratcheted up the anticipation immediately, peeling rubber and screaming, "Yahoo, Irene, here we come!"

It took five minutes to hit country from downtown Warner.

"How far is this place, Eddie?"

"Just out in the country, J.T. Why does it matter?"

J.T. and Beu had lost their bearings as soon as the car left the main highway.

"Eddie, we just gonna walk up to her house and knock or something?"

"Won't even have to do that. Irene will see our car lights down on the road and know you're on the way. You walk about a hundred and fifty yards to the house, say 'Irene, Irene' very quietly, and next thing you know, you're in Paradise."

"I don't think I'd know what to do then, Eddie."

"Irene will show you all that, buddy boy."

"Does she know our names?"

"Damn, J.T., you ask too many questions. Just relax, enjoy the whole experience, okay? It's not your name she's interested in, numbnuts."

"Why don't you guys go up first?"

"For the hundredth time, J.T., she don't like older fellas. Once they get past sixteen, Irene just has *no interest.*"

"Well, I don't understand that."

"Never try to understand women, J.T. In the history of the world, no one's ever done it, and you sure ain't gonna be the first. Why don't you just sit still like Beu and try not to think of Irene *too* much, so you'll be able to walk to the house normal like."

Beu had not spoken a word since they entered the car and didn't still.

"You boys like girls with the big headlights, don't you? Well, Irene could breastfeed India. Just two of her many great features."

"This is really scary, Eddie. You sure her husband's gone?"

"Sure I'm sure. Don't worry about it. This is gonna be a ton of fun, especially for me and Poot."

"You and Poot!"

"Yeah, you know, thinking about what you're doing up there. Feeling good about giving you this, this *gift.* One thing, if Irene asks you to stay the night, you beg off. Poot and me can't come back out here tomorrow.

We're willin' to wait a couple of hours tonight, but that's the end of the deal for us."

Poot pulled the Ford off onto yet another road, drove slowly down it, then stopped. He flicked his headlights off twice, then turned them off completely along with the idling motor. J.T. and Beu were still lost, but that wasn't a part of their thought process at the moment.

"Can you see the house up there?" Eddie asked. There was no moon, but both boys could make out a shape, dark and foreboding but bright with promise.

"Yeah," said J.T. Beu remained silent.

"All right, you know what to do, cowboys. Commence to ride!"

J.T. and Beu got out of the car. They crossed the road, J.T. looking nervously both ways as if checking traffic on a busy city street. No husband roaring down the road to intercept them, he determined. The one-lane road up to the house was rutted and ill kept, with weeds three and four feet high growing beside it. *Feller should stay home and fix up his place,* thought J.T. They looked ahead. Irene had left on zero lights, not even a candle. When they got closer, they saw the house. It looked in disrepair as well. Not even curtains. But then Eddie had said Irene wasn't much of a housekeeper, given the number of fifteen- to sixteen-year-old boys hereabouts. Beu touched J.T. on the arm. J.T. jumped back and gasped. Beu held one finger to his pursed lips. "Shhh, J.T., quiet." Twenty steps later, Beu broke the silence. "Irene," he said softly. "Irene?" No answer.

J.T. summoned up the courage for a more manly and deep, "Irene."

At that moment there was a loud banging of wood, perhaps Irene's furniture being shattered, and a madman's scream of rage, "All right, you sons of bitches. I finally caught you. You are *dead!*" The scream was followed by a shotgun blast. The two boys heard the buckshot rocket above their heads. They turned and bounded toward the road and the car. Another scream, "You're not getting away this time!" Another shotgun blast sent pellets tearing through the weeds to their right. J.T. expected to feel the buckshot enter his back and pictured his bloody collapse. What would Mama say! His brother fighting Japs on some island and he's the one who gets shot. If he lived, how would he explain Irene to Mama.

"Don't stop!" yelled Beu. "Shit, where's the car? Those bastards have run for it!" Both boys turned down the road the way they had come in, came to the last turnoff and kept running. J.T. felt like he could run all night, the mixture of fear and adrenaline a bottomless reservoir of energy. At last they reached the highway. They had heard no threatening sounds or speeding vehicles since they left Irene's yard. Finally they began to walk, heading toward town, looking back to see what followed. When the occasional car came by, the boys ducked into the drainage ditch alongside the highway. They had been silent since they got to the paved road. Beu was limping slightly and J.T.'s pants leg was chaffing his leg. He noticed it was wet and there was a squishing sound coming from his shoe.

"Just our luck the guy was home, huh, Beu? Otherwise ... whoa."

"There was no Irene, J.T."

"What do you mean?"

"I was thinking about it all the way out. Why are those guys so good to us? We don't even know them, hardly. I was fixin' to say take us back to town, but I didn't."

"You mean ..."

"That's right, J.T., no Irene, no husband in Fort Worth. Just two dumbass, cretin, peckerwood freshmen falling for somethin'."

"It *might* have been true, Beu. Anyways, we're sophomores."

"Look at us, J.T. We're walkin' five miles into town, you've pissed your pants, I turned my ankle in one of those ruts, and somewhere back in town a bunch of seniors are laughing their asses off about how we flew down that road, just about crappin' our jeans ever time that shotgun went off. So stupid, so dumb, so cretin."

"It *was* exciting, though, Beu."

"Hell it was."

"Maybe, just maybe, there *is* an Irene, Beu."

"Yeah, and she's back there humping Santa Claus and the Easter Bunny. I swear, J.T., sometimes you seem about twelve years old."

Chapter 11

THE TEXAS SUN BAKED the prison campgrounds where some sought shade under the overhang of the barracks while others pushed their luck and stretched out on blankets laid completely under the buildings and past the concrete supporting posts. This was a forbidden area for prisoners, but today the guards only yawned down their boredom from above and did not shout for the loungers to move out into better sight lines. Prisoners were allowed to move tables and chairs outside from the barracks and mess hall for board games and conversation on weekends. It was Sunday, and most of the men were in the compound yards, shirtless, some wearing shorts of German desert issue while others wore cut-down uniform trousers whose knees had, like their wearers, known better days.

Otto sat in a chair with a towel draped over his shoulders while Klaus cut his hair. Scissors could be checked out from the guards for this purpose but must be used outside and checked in immediately after use, then checked out again by other "barbers." The blunt-pointed cutting shears could not be taken inside the barracks. Few got their hair cut this way, instead opting for the base barbers who came in on some Saturdays and would give three- to five-minute cuts to dozens of men in a morning. Recent arrivals who had been shaved and deloused only days before needed neither service.

The compound was alive with activity. On the dirt soccer field a form of European football was being played. Otto had moved his chair to watch but did not like what he saw.

"Move, move, verdammt, spread out—stupid Dummköpfe, where did they learn to play Fussball?" Otto asked.

"Go down and play mit them, Otto, if they distress you so."

"No, then I would end up coaching, or perhaps punching someone. My town team played better than that."

"They're just prisoners getting some exercise, mein Freund. You can't take that seriously."

Otto was not to be placated. "I call that grenade football, all bunched up. You were a gunner, Klaus, so you didn't have infantry training. In the infantry, our sergeants would scream at us—'Stay spaced, don't bunch up, one grenade would kill you all.' Look at that mess, fifteen men in a little flock trying to kick one ball. No passing, no passing. I wish I had a grenade. Gib ab Dummköpfe!"

"I find it funny, Otto, you comparing football to warfare. Spacing, spreading out, seems so *logical* today. Ancient armies simply lined up side by side and walked or rode right into the enemy's spears or swords or guns. And then imagine only thirty years ago, *thirty years,* they dug trenches and fought from them, leaving their dugouts to charge directly into enemy fire, *had not* learned a thing. And then the German Army redefined it all: no fortresses, defended until death, no Maginot line—just swift, mobile, deadly armies covering a hundred miles a day. The Blitzkrieg! We were a great army, Otto, but stretched too far. Africa, France, Russia—too far. And North Africa, that useless shithole. I know you say it was important, but I was there two years and I saw not *one thing* worth fighting over. Empire building, that's what we were doing.

"I've told you, Klaus, it was for the oil, the Suez Canal, worthy objectives having nothing to do with empire. The empire may have been why the Italians joined us, however. They had to get into the fight so some of the spoils could be theirs. If they waited too long, it would all be Germany's and they would be a standing army that never got past downtown Pompeii."

"Otto, you should have been a general. You have a military mind; you make logical, tough sense of it all."

"No, I am just a desert rat to Rommel's Desert Fox. Snatched from my little sand castle like a child, led away with my thumb in my mouth, in disgrace. No potential for leading an army can be seen in my demise. From wadi jumper to farm hand. Brilliant!"

"But you marched proudly through Benghazi in triumph. Can't take that away from us, the cheers, the banquets of food and drink. And remember being a part of Rommel's great maneuvers, feint here, strike there. Mount airplane engines on trucks to blow dust that made it appear an entire division was on the move. Remember, Otto?"

"Yes, I remember all that. I also remember Benghazi. I'm sure the British received the same treatment when they came through. Benghazi was practicing the politics of survival." Klaus paused in his cutting.

"What's the future, Otto? If our soldiers free us you would likely be hung, and me also, for fraternizing with you."

"Yes, likely."

"I think I will escape, Otto, maybe just long enough to have a woman. You could escape again, eh? Go with me?"

"I did not *escape*, Klaus. I am not crazy, and I am going nowhere. How many times must I explain?"

"All right, I will change the subject from escape, you from football. Let's be two old men on the park bench and talk about the passersby. You enjoy that, I know. Is there anyone in Camp 67 who has escaped your scrutiny and analysis, professor?"

"I *have* made one analysis today. You are *not* a barber."

"Danke schön."

"Did you pick the nits from my hair? I do not want to be deloused and shaved again."

"Don't worry, Herr Becker, full service job for you."

"Look down there," said Otto.

"The Red Cross has given us a wrestling mat, you notice, Klaus. But it is hard and of a rough texture.

"Some are using it today, regardless."

"We need boxing gloves, Klaus. That would let the steam off."

"Ja, you could challenge von Hoffmann. I would waive my canteen privileges to see that."

"That would be like Max Schmeling fighting Willie Pep, Klaus. What does the good Obersturmführer weigh, you think, sixty-five kilos? It would be my pleasure, of course, but not sporting. Perhaps we could fight like I had my students settle arguments when it got to the punching stage. We tied an inflated inner tube around their waist, gave them boxing gloves, and ...."—Otto laughs at the memory—" ... very, very funny, trying to reach the opponent's chin, bouncing back when tube met tube. I hadn't thought about that in some time. The good ole days, as the Americans would say."

"There's Wagner. You could challenge him," said Klaus motioning toward a huge, muscled prisoner arm wrestling a man with half his mass. Wagner worked at the base loading docks removing supplies and huge crates of airplane motor parts from trucks servicing the base. Hollywood would have called it type casting. Wagner disdainfully kept both his and his opponent's arms in an upright position while with his left hand he took a cigarette from the pack on the table, placed it in his mouth, then scratched a match across the table top, lit the cigarette, inhaled, then viciously slammed the hapless man's arm to the table.

Klaus nodded toward Wagner. "Eh, Otto, next?"

"Perhaps not," said Otto.

"Where is Hahn going?" Klaus asked, as a slight, stooped prisoner was being escorted out of the compound by a guard.

"He has a visitor, a cousin from Cincinnati in the state of Ohio. She borrowed gas stamps from her relatives and friends to make the journey! There again, Klaus, the bizarre Americans helping a girl to go visit an enemy soldier. Why would they be complicit in such an act? Strange people, mystifying country, soft as Jell-O with steel rod running down its middle."

"What about your uncle in Fredericksburg, Otto? Do you think he will ever visit you?"

"I don't think so. From my memories of him, I couldn't say, but at one time he did write my father expressing his concern about the Führer's intentions for Germany. I would not put him in a poor position by making contact. Perhaps after the war I will see him."

"Look, Otto, Jürgen is still wearing his PW shirt." Jürgen was the oldest prisoner in Camp 67, having reached his fiftieth birthday shortly after his arrival. Jürgen had somehow removed the painted "O" from POW.

What was left was the familiar PW for *Pensionierte Wehrmacht* or *Retired Soldier*. He delighted in the attention he received for his cleverness.

"PW. I think we are all retired soldiers, Klaus, just not voluntary." Klaus smiled and waved at Jürgen, who waved back, happy for the recognition of his claim to fame.

"We could truly write a book, Otto. There are three hundred interesting stories here, I am sure. You have Schafer there, who claims he and twenty other young men of German parents were forced onto a ship in Peru, taken to Germany, and conscripted into the army. He'll tell you the entire story in Spanish, if you wish him to prove his origins."

"And they say Wagner was in prison and given release if he would fight."

"Our arm wrestler Wagner?"

"Ja."

"And Kruger, you forgot Kruger, Klaus. The pathetic Kruger."

"I didn't forget him, Otto. Chapter Twelve of our book, *Wolfgang Kruger*, who never stops whining that he is an officer who had his papers, medals, and all identification stolen on the ship over. When he could produce only his name, the Americans listed him as Private Wolfgang Kruger, and so he has remained. A sad story, indeed. My ass bleeds for him."

"There's Bachman, who collects the lizards and the armadillo and whatever else he has in his little zoo over there. No snakes! I will personally thrash him if he brings snakes into this compound. Hardly a day goes by I don't kill one on the farm. I am very afraid of snakes, Klaus. They scare me more than bullets or those unexploded bombs you play with each day."

"Yes, I know your fear there, mein Freund. I don't come in contact with them where I work. I don't think they like loud noise."

"I am reading a book, Klaus, one of those the Red Cross brought in—all in English, no German novels yet. It's called *The Grapes of Wrath*, by a John Steinbeck."

"Sounds like a Jew name, Otto. I never heard of him or the book. Perhaps that is the reason."

"I don't know if he's a Jew, Klaus. If he is, I'm sure I'll hear from von Hoffmann on it. It's about people like my farmer boss. I am learning about the men of this province."

There were several moments of silence.

"Are we all out of news, old man on the bench?" Klaus asked.

"Let's see. The colonel still talks only to Captain Müeller, refuses to accept von Hoffmann's claim to leadership. It makes von Hoffmann furious, as does everything, but it is not Müeller's fault. I do think Colonel Payne likes having von Hoffmann here. He doesn't have to provide discipline, it's all internal and neatly wrapped up for him. For instance, he has done nothing about Richter, and when Bauer was beaten so badly he was taken to the infirmary—nothing was heard from Colonel Payne."

"I don't think he would put up with murder though, Otto."

"Why do you mention murder?"

"Perhaps von Hoffmann goes too far and his victim dies, or the victim retaliates in such a manner that we lose the services of our mighty SS Obersturmführer, *permanently.*"

"Interesting thought, Herr *Friseur.* Now give me your mirror so I can see how handsome you have made me."

Chapter 12

THE NEXT DAY OTTO and his fellow McConnell farm workers were pulled to work on base, a maintenance project involving the repairs on the outer fence that surrounded Camp 67. It seemed to be a more cosmetic than security driven project, likely some officer's idea that an escape was imminent and a few extra strands of barbed wire and post reinforcement would thwart any attempt the prisoners had in mind.

It was the first time Otto had been close to the fence since he helped build it. The work was no more impressive than when they had dug the postholes and poured the cement months before. He remembered the building of the camp as the most pleasant period of his internment, if the words "prison" and "pleasant" could ever coexist. The prisoners ate in the airmen's mess, were treated with courtesy, the work hard but with no demands or threats to push past one's normal capacity.

Six months had elapsed between the time Otto arrived at Camp 67 and his debarkation at McLean, Texas, one of over three thousand prisoners who would eventually be held at the facility there. The Afrika Korps group had arrived, a tired and ragged bunch attempting to display a proud, arrogant bearing in keeping with their elite status as they were marched from the train through the town to the waiting trucks. The crowd that watched knew nothing of their unit's history, being drawn to watch out of curiosity rather than admiration. Some of the people seemed to look at them with some sympathy, mostly women who may have thought of them as someone's son, husband, or brother rather than an enemy soldier.

Camp 67 was to be built at the Army Air Force bombardier base at Warner, Texas, a branch camp, one of dozens being thrown up across the U.S. A few prisoner groups simply moved into vacated CCC camps, but the majority of the facilities had to be built from scratch, and quickly, as the thousands of Axis soldiers poured into the country. The branch camps were created to relieve overcrowding at the large camps and to distribute the farm labor across the state. Camp 67 would house over three hundred prisoners. Otto never learned why he was included with men who had building skills. He had none. Likely he looked to be a strong, healthy man suited to swinging a pick and manning a shovel.

To Otto the Warner area looked pretty much the same as McLean, but he had convinced himself that a camp of three hundred would be more tolerable were he able to stay once the construction was completed.

The prisoners had been transported from McLean to Camp 67 in a school bus, or what had been a school bus. Two guards rode with them. Neither seemed to consider their cargo volatile or dangerous in any way. The guard with the backseat to himself read a magazine, seldom looking up, while his partner sat in front engrossed in a conversation with the driver on war and wayward women. Two rest stops were provided, unlike the trip to Casablanca.

The barracks builders lived in five-man tents set to one end of the working site. This "prison" was enclosed by hastily assembled rolls of barbed wire, sans posts, making it as insecure a prison camp as had ever been erected.

Otto had moved his bed gear outside at night to avoid the smell and snoring of his tent mates, as well as to indulge his preference for the outdoors developed over two years without a roof over his head. He was amused at this newfound propensity having grown up in a family for which the sunlight and moonlight were conditions they traversed from building to car or train. The Texas night sky was beautiful, filled with diamondlike stars that had been obscured by the smoke and dust of North Africa. Wasn't there a song about the stars in Texas? He couldn't imagine *any* music that could enhance his nightly experience.

He and his fellow prisoners, under the direction of American civilians, built quarters for three hundred fifty men. Four buildings were erected, two for lower-ranked soldiers, the other for NCOs and officers, and then a mess hall and kitchen. The separation by rank was one of many Geneva Convention requirements adhered to by the U.S. and frequently ignored in other countries involved in the war. The foot soldier buildings held three hundred prisoners, the NCO and officer quarters fifty. The military bases selected as branch camps had been assured they would have to take no more than four hundred prisoners, but the tents were relegated to handy storage nevertheless. The buildings were set on four-foot concrete stilts, providing the guards a clear view underneath the buildings, discouraging tunneling. Between the two main barracks buildings a laundry room was built and equipped with wash tubs, rubbing boards, and heavy bristled brushes. Wire clotheslines were strung along the area behind the barracks in full sight of Tower 2. The structures were spare and meant to be temporary. Windows opened for air, but the six-inch opening made escape through that crevice unlikely. The floors were unfinished hardwood, the walls black tar paper, and the roofs low-grade asphalt shingling. A foot locker was provided for each prisoner, as well as an open shelf and hook that served as their closet. A pot-bellied stove with a tin flue pipe sat in the middle of the building but would become unnecessary as the Texas spring morphed into summer. Completing the décor were four small tables with an equal number of chairs each placed precisely at equal distances on the barracks floor. Showers and a latrine were located at the end of each building. The debut of the showers had been a celebratory event for the tent-dwelling prisoners. The last building completed was a mess hall that seated two hundred men and required two serving shifts. Two hundred fifty men had been sent to Camp 67 in the first transfer, with the camp growing to capacity in late April and early May. Per Geneva Convention, the NCOs and officers were not required to work and few did. The prisoner routine had been set and not changed to this day, one of 6 a.m. wakeup, breakfast, and then to work for those not exempted. Prisoners were returned at around 6 p.m. with dinner at 7 and lights out at 9:30 except those in the latrine. The guard detail locked the barracks at 11 p.m. Von Hoffmann had protested locked barracks as a death trap in case of fire, and it was a battle he won. Prisoners were warned, however, that should they set foot outside the building after the barracks were darkened they would be shot. Colonel Payne said that he would follow all Geneva Convention rules. The rules said the officers didn't have to work but it didn't say they could not be fed last, and so they were. This was Obersturmführer von Hoffmann's third filed protest after his arrival, but it was ignored.

The prison complex included a dirt field, for recreation. The construction crew had built netless soccer goals which stood at each end of the field. There was no flag pole in the complex or anywhere near. This, too, was by design. At the main camp in McLean, the Germans had created a Nazi flag they ran up the pole to commemorate Hitler's birthday on April 20. They had then cut the lines and greased the pole, creating a half day's work by camp soldiers to remove it. Two ten-foot fences surrounded the compact prison complex, consisting of an "inner fence" and an "outer fence," which the work crew was servicing today. The two were separated by twenty-five yards of "No Man's Land," the entire barbed wire fence, including the two gates, topped with rolled barbed wire, the poles metal and curved inward to discourage climbing. Guard towers at all four corners of the enclosure were manned round the clock by a soldier with a mounted machine gun on a swivel base, a sidearm, and a stacked and loaded carbine rifle.

A spotlight capable of a three hundred sixty degree rotation and a swivel sitting stool completed the furnishing. In the early days of the camp suspicious prisoner activity was nil and the tower duty deadly dull. Spotting the light on coyotes and rabbits outside the fence, then dispatching them with the carbine, became a favorite pastime for the guards. An amplified sound system was the guard's final tool, an otherworld thunderbolt from high above the grounds designed to put fear in a potential escapee's heart and assure that every soul in the camp was awakened.

As Otto worked he again noted the vulnerable spots in the fence and the areas he deemed to be difficult to monitor by the guards in the towers. Information he had no immediate plans to use but life in the camp was profoundly a day-by-day existence sometimes propelling the pacifist to activist overnight.

Chapter 13

GREEN COTTON STALKS STOOD in perfect rows, bolls not formed, the crop a little leafy this year which would make the pulling more difficult in the fall. It was bumper-like, to be sure, if only there were no heavy rains or hail that would hammer the bolls and open cotton into mud balls beneath a stripped, bare stalk. The two months from this stage to the wagons lined up outside the gin were critical. Enough rain for the cotton's health, but not enough to alter the yield.

The rains to this point had been generous to all living things. The cotton flourished, as did the Johnson grass, jimson weed, Russian thistle, ragweed, goatheads, and sunflowers. They all vied for the nourishment of the soil and the rain's kiss, both meant for King Cotton. Like Camp 67, Ed McConnell's farm was full of an enemy of another kind. Eleven POWs and J.T. Graham walked the rows, sharpened hoes wielded in gloved hand, eliminating the weeds, some healthier than the cotton they threatened. None of the men had ever seen cotton growing nor pulled the fluffy bloom from its stalk.

Sergeant Preston sat above the rows' ends on a raised chair he had built, six feet in height, with slatted steps for accessing his perch. He had added a plywood top and another piece to keep the sun from the back of his neck. The chair was moved from place to place by the prisoners, west-facing in the morning, east in the afternoon. A folded cotton sack taped to the chair served as his cushion.

On the road, a half mile distant from the field, a car stopped and a figure emerged. He jumped the ditch, climbed between strands of barbed wire and ran toward the workers.

"Hey, it's Beu—hey, Beu!"

Beu waved as he leaped the cotton rows.

"What's going on, Beu, come to help?"

"No, and don't try to pull a Tom Sawyer on me neither, J.T. I just came out to watch and give you a ride home later."

"You'd have to wait until I pick up the slop. Today's a pickup day. Actually need to go pretty soon so I have someone to help me unload when I get back."

"I'll go with you."

"Got a base pass?"

"Sure, my dad got me one."

"What for?"

"So's I'd have a pass, that's what for."

Sergeant Preston peered down at Beu and addressed him with some displeasure in his hoarse voice. "Ed's not going to let you stick around if he sees you, Beu." Beu ignored him.

"I just ran over a huge rattlesnake up on the road. Cut him right in two with my tire. One end was rattling, the other one still bitin' out with that forked tongue." Beu looked to Otto for a reaction.

"Nah," said Otto with disgust.

"He's just foolin' with you, Mr. Becker. I told him how you hated snakes."

"You said *afraid* of snakes, J.T."

"You a joker boy, hey, Beu?"

"Well, plenty of people play them on me."

"Won't do it again if you tell us why they call you Crazy Otto."

"German Army secret, Beuford. If I told you, these men with the sharp hoes would kill me."

"Aw, don't treat us like kids. Tell us."

"Someday I'll tell Kumpel. Then perhaps he'll tell you, or maybe I'll tell him not to share with Joker Boy."

"All right, break time," Sergeant Preston yelled. The men headed for the water coolers covered with a tarp to minimize the sun's intensity. Four communal dippers hung from the cooler lid for the use of all the workers, including J.T. There was no spout for delivery to the dippers so they dipped, drank, and passed the utensil to the next person in queue.

"Boy, I could use a soda pop," said J.T., submerging his dipper into the water that once floated a block of ice but was now approaching the outside temperature.

"Beer, beer is what we need!" said Otto, then to his fellow POWs, "eine Bierflasche, ja! eine Bierflasche!" The prisoners repeated his yell, "Bier, Bier!"

One prisoner was butchering an American pop song as he waited to drink. "Give me five minutes more, only five minutes more."

"She said you only need three, Gerhardt," said another POW who sat nearby. Gerhardt laughed and started, "You are my sunshine, my only ..."

Beu was amazed. "You German fellers know American songs?"

"Of course," said Otto. "That's all we get to hear. We have one radio. It gets three stations, American music all day, all night too I imagine."

"Do you like it?" asked J.T.

"We would like the German music but this is all we get. Better than nothing, but your songs are crazier than Crazy Otto. What is, 'Mares eat oats and does eat oats and little lambs eat ivy!' A song?"

"My mom likes that one," said Beu.

"And 'Accentuate the positive, eliminate the negative.' I understand the message, but a song! 'You Are My Sunshine' is okay. Gerhardt likes that one, eh Gerhardt?"

"You are my sunshine ..."

"No, Gerhardt. I didn't ask you to sing it. Sometimes I forget to use German, then sometimes same with English."

"We like your Mills Brothers. What's the song?"

"Paper Doll?" said J.T.

"Yes, yes, that one."

"But our very best favorite—all the men here can sing it—can you guess? No? How about you, Sergeant of the Yukon? Nein, nein? Okay, I tell the men in German and then we sing—okay?"

Otto raised his hand like a conductor.

"Oh, give me land

"Lots of land

"Under starry skies above

"DON'T FENCE ME IN!"

The POWs laughed loudly and repeated, "Don't fence me in."

"You like that one, Joker boy?"

"Sure," said Beu. "But there's a song you Germans need to learn. It's called *Old MacDonald Had A Farm*, only J.T. and me substitute Old McConnell for Old MacDonald. Get it?"

"Why should we learn that song?" Otto looked from Beu to J.T.

"'Cause Mr. Mac would like to hear it, huh J.T.?"

"Aw, Beu."

Sergeant Preston interrupted. "You boys are cruisin' for a bruisin', fooling with Ed. You know he's got a bad temper."

"The farmer wouldn't like the song?" said Otto. "You mean he is not a *daddy-o?*"

"No, and he ain't a *real cool cat,* either," said Preston.

"Okay, Sergeant Preston. We'll just teach it to Otto and the Germans and they can sing it back at the barracks. Help me out, J.T."

"Okay, goes like this." Beu started, J.T. joined in.

"Old McConnell had a farm

"Eee-yi-eee-yi-oh

"And on this farm he had some pigs

"Eee-yi-eee-yi-oh

"With an oink, oink here and an oink, oink there

Here an oink, there an oink, everywhere an oink, oink

"Old McConnell had a farm

"Eee-yi-eee-yi-oh!"

Beu and J.T. sang the one verse through with the prisoners until Otto said, "I think they have it, Kumpel."

"So to sing this song would make the farmer happy? Is that right?" Otto smiled up at Sergeant Preston, who shook his head.

"One thing Ed doesn't have is a sense of humor."

"Okay, Kumpel. Thank you and the Joker Boy for the new song. We will practice until we have German perfection."

"*Pistol* perfect, as ole Eddie Jackson would say. Right, J.T.?"

"Beu, I need to git. This is the time I usually leave for the base. You still comin'?"

"Sure am, let's go. Pig slop waits for no man, right J.T.?"

"Bye, fellers, see you tomorrow." J.T. shouldered his hoe and lunch box and headed for the barn.

Chapter 14

THE LANDINGS AT NORMANDY had shaken the prisoners more than they wished to admit. Until that point the war had been fought in other people's countries. There had been the bombings of German factories but no troops had set foot on German soil, but now the Allies were in France, only a few hundred kilometers from the Fatherland. Prisoners talked in whispers about the invasion, what to believe from the American radio and soldiers who held them captive. Those who believed the American accounts were careful not to express that belief. Toeing the Nazi Party line was a healthier option than siding with Otto Becker, whom they viewed as either deserving of his "crazy" title or borderline suicidal. The Nazis told the men again and again that it was all lies, propaganda meant to demoralize, to weaken any resolve which might take the form of physical resistance or escape. Von Hoffmann claimed he was in contact with the High Command in Berlin who verified his claims about American propaganda and demanded, through him, that all German military personnel remain ready for an uprising involving all prison camps in America. He told them German and Italian prisoners outnumbered the U.S. military presence at home, that a plan to turn those numbers into an insurrection was being made as he spoke.

The date was July 23. American newscasts and newspapers, given freely to the prisoners on such occasions, had reported an attempt on the life of Adolph Hitler three days before. Von Hoffmann had gathered all the men into the enlisted barracks to address this report. For once the soldiers were eager to be subjected to a von Hoffmann tirade, given the new subject, one that had been received with mixed emotions among the prisoners.

Von Hoffmann paced like an actor ready to impart the key line in the play but determined to command the stage with his presence as long as he could before its delivery. Only the sound of glove slapping hand and hobnailed boots echoing off the wood floor could be heard.

"The Führer is *not dead!*" he shouted. "No cowardly traitors are capable of harming this great man, and those who have tried are being dealt with as we stand here today, in a manner that will strike terror into the heart of any man who has even such a *thought* again."

"The American newspapers have not said whether he was harmed as yet, Obersturmführer. Where do you get such good news?" said Otto Becker.

"Shut up, Becker," someone yelled from the crowd of prisoners.

Otto continued. "We were told not to believe the propaganda from the Americans about Normandy. Why are you telling us to believe your story of the attempt on the Führer's life?"

"Becker, how dare you interrupt my address to the men? How dare you question an officer of the German Army? Insubordination! Disrespect to a German officer! Becker, you are a dead man when you are returned to Germany, *if not sooner!*"

"I would be executed? For what? I am just Otto Becker, the soldier without a war. All that is left is Becker the man. I exist here each grimy day with other men, men who wish to be able to ask a simple question without having their life threatened."

"A simple question about source, Obersturmführer."

"Did you hear your information on your radio which receives direct messages from the SS in Berlin, eager to answer your every question? Or perhaps the secret coded messages you send out in your letters. Did they inform you by special mail, flown in just three days after the attempt on the Führer's life?"

"I'm warning you, Becker. *Halte den Mund!*"

"I will shut up, sir, when you answer questions that are legitimate and need an answer. I have seen General Rommel have many conversations with foot soldiers such as myself, and *you* are too important to be questioned?"

"Take Private Becker into custody," von Hoffmann said. Three men moved toward him but were blocked by others who stood between them. Shoving and shouting began. Loyalties previously hidden seemed to surface. The communists sided with Otto's friends and some who Otto had thought to be Nazis shouted and were shouted at in return.

"Perhaps you should *personally* arrest me, Obersturmführer. But before you do, why don't you share with the men the reason your uniform is untattered and clean. These men fought for their country, some five years, and you, Lieutenant? Tell them about your combat experience that gives you the right to bully these men. Armans Müeller saw combat and he is a captain. Why are you in command here?"

"Becker, I will kill you personally!"

"Brave soldiers have tried that, and I am here. Men, do you know what our gallant lieutenant's job was before he was captured? He supervised a work camp for Jews! Why is an SS man needed at a simple work camp? He has not fired one shot, not seen one day of combat. But I think he has killed many people. Is that not true, Lieutenant? Were your duties to kill Jews in the work camps? Unarmed Jews? Women and children Jews?"

"Den Mund halten!"

"Easy, mein Freund, easy," Klaus pleaded, holding Otto's arm and pulling him back.

"Tell us about Dachau, Auschwitz, and Treblinka, good Obersturmführer."

"Where did you hear those names, Becker? Every word you utter is treason, a crime against Germany! You are a disgrace to all who are in this room. You lie!"

"How do we even know you are SS, von Hoffmann? If I am lying about your war record, please tell the men what you have done for the Fatherland, the German Army, for these men. We would all like to hear it." Otto's face was crimson with rage. Klaus continued to hold him from translating his verbiage into action. Otto delivered the final insult.

"Perhaps you are a Jew! That's it! What better way to hide it than joining the SS!"

Von Hoffmann charged Becker. All sides lost perspective and control, giving way to a riot of brawling and shouting. Otto was pummeled with shoves and blows and could not make his way to von Hoffmann nor the Obersturmführer to him.

The shouting turned to blows, crude weapons of wood and metal appeared, one rioting side difficult to tell from the other. The barracks door flew open, a whistle blew, and guards armed with clubs waded into the melee.

Otto lay in his bunk, eyes opened, body still twitching from the adrenal stimulation from hours before. Would he sleep at all, given von Hoffmann's threats? He heard the midnight changing of the guard outside the barracks and tried to think of his wife, his son, the school, Dresden, but morbid thoughts ruled the night. There was no doubt they would try to kill him, tonight or another of their choice. Most people are surprised by death, don't see it coming, never consider its dark visit. What percentage experience the final days of a long illness or reach an age that counts down life by days or hours? No, most are surprised but never get to tell you *how* surprised they were. If von Hoffmann had his wish, he would have been marched out and shot immediately. There would be no surprises for Crazy Otto, who once again had demonstrated the appropriateness of that label. Otto tried to lighten his thoughts by playing out his death scene, one in which he paced the barracks, slapping borrowed SS gloves in his hand, delivering his last words to a rapt audience, to whom he then waved as he was led out the door. The scene played out quickly when he recalled actually having heard the *last* words of a battlefield comrade. He had held his friend in his arms when he died. His last words were, "No loss, Otto." Otto had dropped tears upon the man's face. What loss me? Did having a wife and son make me more of a loss than his friend who had neither? Since death is inevitable, does the time or method really matter? To have von Hoffmann make those decisions *did* matter. Not acceptable! Nein! Nein! Nein!

Chapter 15

LATER, OTTO WOULD THINK back with embarrassment at his puny resistance to the attack. It seemed a part of a dream, the blows raining down on him, not reality. He remembered kicking out and swinging his fist at a shadowy target, delivering only a glancing blow. Then darkness.

The base infirmary consisted of two wards: the larger one, in theory, for the base personnel; the smaller, for prisoners. Given the disparity in numbers, part of the prisoner ward usually housed spillover from the pilots, crews, and support personnel in need of bed care. White standup screens separated the two groups but the same American doctors attended both. At the McLean camp, two German doctors and a dentist were among the prisoners and assisted in the medical care for the three thousand prisoners. No medical personnel had been among the transfers or new arrivals at Camp 67. Prisoners *did* work as orderlies. There were four nurses among the permanent base staff, but they did not serve in the prisoner ward except during operations.

A man in a white jacket, with a stethoscope draped over a barrel chest, entered the area where Otto lay. He came to Otto's bed.

"Good afternoon, Private Becker. I'm Dr. Whitehead."

"And a major, as well."

"Yes, that too. How are you feeling?"

"I'm searching for a part of me that is not sore."

"They told me you speak English, and very well I might add, with only a trace of accent. Yes, I imagine you are sore. There don't seem to be many areas of your body without bruises. You have by my count a concussion, two broken ribs, lacerations of the face and arms, and severe bruising of the torso. Any place I forgot?"

"I'm still searching."

"I understand some of your fellow soldiers came forward and stopped the attack. You probably owe them your life."

Otto tried to mask his look of surprise. Von Hoffmann wanted to finish it right there, didn't he.

"Well, Private, we will keep you here one more day, then you may return to your barracks confined in bed there for a week, then I'll check you again to see if you are able to return to light duty."

"I'd like to go back to the farm. I would rather be out of doors."

"You're in a hurry to go back to work on a cotton farm? Maybe your head injury is more severe than I thought." Otto did not answer.

"There's a gentleman from the Military Police who wishes to speak with you. Are you up to that?"

"Yes," Otto nodded, then a groaning stretch of his body to the right to see if the man was present.

"I'm right here, Private Becker. Thank you, Doctor."

The Military Police officer looked at Otto with some of the disdain he hadn't seen since the questioning sessions in Casablanca. The officer's nose was hawklike and his coloring could be American Indian. Otto waited for an introduction to Lieutenant Red Cloud or Lightfeather.

"I'm Lieutenant Williams of the U.S. Military Police, Private Becker, Provost Office."

"I don't remember seeing you before, Lieutenant."

"That's because I came down from the camp at McLean."

"All that way to speak to a clumsy prisoner who fell out of his bunk?"

"I'm here to observe, with my own eyes, a man who fell from a bunk eighteen inches high and had to be hospitalized. Must be a medical record of some sort."

"Could you get me a bottle of beer? I'm sure it would loosen my tongue considerably. I could add more information for your medical research if you primed the pump, so to speak."

"There is no beer on this base, as I understand it, Private Becker."

"You don't believe that, do you?"

"From your attitude, I imagine this is going to be a short interview. Will you tell me who gave you this beating?"

"What beating?"

"Doc says they did a very professional job, one that you will remember."

"I fell, I just bruise easily."

"This is not some Bogart movie, Becker. I really don't care much who beat you up so save the tough guy dialogue. This is routine procedure for me. The men who sleep near you say they didn't hear or see a thing. We call that 'Barracks Amnesia.' Seems to affect about a hundred percent of you Germans in these cases."

"I don't remember a thing. If they don't, I don't see how I can help you."

"Did an SS officer named von Hoffmann have anything to do with this?"

"One of my best friends."

"Colonel Payne tells me his name comes up frequently when there's any type of trouble."

"Colonel Payne would know that, not I."

"I don't understand why you men stand by and let a man like that get away with it. In most units I've been in, he would have received a beating in return—or worse."

"You said that, Lieutenant, not me."

"To tell you the truth, I'm really interested in only one thing, that is if you were beaten by our guards. If that is the case, then I would be all ears. Did our guards do this?"

"No, the guards like me. Ask around. They call me Crazy Otto and I have given them a great laugh. I have brought them pleasure."

"I'll do that. Last chance, Becker. Do you wish to make a statement or not?"

"Not."

"Then looks like a long drive and a wasted afternoon. I hope I don't have to return for the burying of your body."

"Don't worry, sir. I shall not be so clumsy next time."

Klaus had pulled up a chair next to Otto's barracks bunk where, a half hour before, he had delivered his lunch, especially prepared for him by Hans. Ever the humorist, Hans had included an ugly and faded weed flower in a jar that served as its vase.

"And why are you not working today, Private Lang?"

"I asked for a day off to be your nursemaid, Private Becker."

"Thank you." The two had spoken little while Otto ate, but when they did it was in English. For unknown reasons, another prisoner lay in his bunk, at the end of the barracks. They were reasonably sure he did not have the language.

"You know I must kill him now, Klaus."

"So, you have already tried to commit suicide by your outburst, now you will complete it by killing von Hoffmann and being hung for doing so? Seven German soldiers were hung, seven, you hear, for killing a man in another camp."

"Do you know this to be fact?"

"It comes from a letter received from that camp, my friend, not from the Americans."

"Otto, does all this have something to do with not hearing from your wife?"

"No."

"Would she be happy you traded your life for that of another German man, no matter how evil?"

"You've said yourself he needs to die."

"Yes, and he will, but not by clownish outbursts such as yours."

"Clownish!"

"All right, not clownish, melodramatic. Like a villain in a bad comic melodrama."

"Von Hoffmann is the villain here, Klaus, a classic one. All he needs is the handlebar mustache."

"And you the prince on the white steed ready to bring him down?"

"You know he must die, Klaus."

"Yes, but don't change the subject. How could you yell at an officer in that manner, even this one? It was not German military. We cannot lose our identity as soldiers, Otto. On that point I must agree with the Obersturmführer.

"Let me see if I hear this right. You would *kill* a German officer, but you don't want to disrespect him?"

"Don't confuse me with logic, Otto. I just mean you didn't have to lose control, I don't think."

"Was I out of control?"

"Yes, you were, but you achieved what you set out to do, I guess. You got the reaction you wanted, didn't you? You *wanted* him to lose it, and he did. At the least, all who were there will never look at von Hoffmann the same. Most of our men here are still in their twenties. Some of their awe, the fear, will be gone. No matter what happens to you, the camp will never be as it was. We are like three camps now: one which would like to see Otto dead, one which would shed no tears if von Hoffmann left us, and quite a few who don't want to be involved on either side."

"Klaus, there was no way to *leak* out what kind of man this pig is. It has to be *said*. Did you see the look on his face when I gave the names of the Jewish camps? It was fright, Klaus. Fright. I think maybe the Obersturmführer thinks about the *possibility* of Germany losing the war and he being returned to face the accounting of his crimes. On one hand, he would like to distance himself from that part of his personal history, and on the other, he is proud of it and would like to do more. I'm both a stand-in for the Jews and also someone who has damaging information, which could be dangerous later."

"Perhaps you give yourself too much credit, my friend. I'm not sure he has any fear of you, only hate. It *is* true that one who had done only good things for his country would not be so insecure. Still, your timing was all wrong on this. On the day the attempt on the Führer's life was the topic, you chose to upstage that event? You should have waited, Otto."

"Why are you trying so hard to give meaning to this, Klaus? Would anyone know about von Hoffmann if I had not spoken up?"

"You have only Fuch's word for all this."

"Fuch risked his life to tell me about von Hoffmann, Klaus. And why did he? Because he's a good soldier, one who joined one army and is sickened to find there may be another army wearing the same uniform but engaged in horrors he can only imagine. And you're worried about a conflict with the news of the Führer? Klaus, I wish they had killed him."

"Don't say that, Otto."

"The Führer has betrayed Germany and our army, Klaus. I'm sure that's why they tried to kill him."

"What do you know for sure, Otto? You are a private, thousands of miles away from the war and military decisions. You have no basis to make statements like that."

"I can't dispute your logic but I can't ignore my instincts either."

"Ahh, Otto. I don't want to argue with you. You are my good and best friend, a brave soldier I not only care about, but respect."

"And I feel the same for you, Private Philosopher. I haven't thanked you. It was you who kept me from being killed, wasn't it?"

"Wagner helped, too."

"Wagner! That must have been interesting."

"There were three or four of them, I think. They all ran, didn't want to be identified, I imagine. None were von Hoffmann, all average sized men. Two left out the door, so they were officers, NCOs, or lived in Barracks Two."

"The guard didn't challenge them?"

"No. The other one or two must have gone back to their bunks. We were just worried about getting you some medical help at that point. We took you outside, *then* the lights came on. I yelled, 'Don't shoot, don't shoot, injured man!' Lucky my English. They came into the compound and took you away. Perhaps they would have stopped beating you as they did with Bauer. Remember we found he had been beaten the next day? Perhaps they would have stopped, who knows?"

"It doesn't matter, Klaus. You stood up, that's all I care."

"And we will settle with von Hoffmann at the best time, a *planned* time, Otto. No more outbursts, *please*."

"Yes, you are right."

"I will distance myself from you in the next days, Otto. I must make peace with von Hoffmann and get closer to him and his thugs. Right now you are that inner tube around my waist, preventing that from happening."

"Why would you want to do that?"

"A *planned* time, the *best* time requires fakes and feints at the enemy's front line. General Rommel taught us that, didn't he? Now give me your tray, bedside service and hand-holding is over."

"Wait, Klaus."

"Ja?"

"You're not just going along to help the revengeful friend, are you?"

"No, killing him is a matter of respect for me, not revenge. Three years of sand and fleas and shrapnel, and this man spits on it. He has not earned the right to spit on the Afrika Korps." Klaus took the tray, looked defiantly around the barracks, and turned to leave. "And we thought we were through with war!"

Otto lay back on the extra pillows supplied by the hospital orderly. Klaus was a man of his word, but Otto couldn't help feeling a degree of regret that Klaus's anger may have been more a result of his bad behavior than von Hoffmann's "matter of respect." Klaus was sure to not like his next confrontation with the *bantam bastard*, which Otto planned for the day he returned to duty.

Otto was walking with no pain now and could have done light duty in the barracks, but he wanted to make the decision of when. For the benefit of his lone barracks mate, Otto got up and hobbled to the latrine, expressing nonexistent pain as he did so.

Chapter 16

ALMA GRAHAM CAUGHT THE bus to the base a full two hours before J.T. and returned home equally earlier. Busses ran every thirty minutes at peak hours and were usually full on both of Mrs. Graham's rides since a number of civilian personnel shared her six to two schedule, including her fellow mess hall workers. J.T.'s morning bus was lightly peopled, while the seats on his five or six o'clock return carriers were full of airmen some of whom stood shoulder to shoulder in the aisle hanging onto the bar above the seats. Those seated smoked, while a sign near the driver said Standing Passengers No Smoking. J.T. figured about 90 percent of the people in the world smoked, or so it seemed. Beu was taking up the habit. J.T. had tried one draw, then began a coughing fit that Beu had said "lasted 'bout an hour." Earlier that year, J.T. had tried chewing tobacco and threw up. Grandma dipped snuff and spat into a coffee can, which J.T. found disgusting, but familiar.

Alma's mind was on the mail as it was every day on the ride home. Each day a silent prayer that in a jungle somewhere Thad would be able to safely sit down and write a letter. In her revelry she didn't notice the blond boy with a lunch pail waiting for the bus to stop. The unscheduled stop drew her attention to the door as the boy entered. J.T. immediately took notice of the woman waving him to the empty seat beside her. He walked sheepishly to the spot and sat gently onto it, ready for the question that came right on cue.

"What are you doing going home this early?"

"Mr. Mac told me to go, 'Go on home,' he said."

"Why?"

I don't know, *really*. He just said I was as useless as a screen door on a submarine so I might as well go on home. That's all he said."

"Well, you must have done something."

"Can we just talk about this when we get home?"

"We surely will."

"Mr. Mac sent you some fruit and vegetables," said J.T., motioning to the paper sack he held.

"You mean he kicked you off the farm and then sent a sack of food?"

"Well, he gave me the stuff *before* he told me to go home. Mama, why don't you bring stuff home from the base? There's a lot of food wasted there. I know, I pick it up."

"They don't allow it, Son, and I'm glad. I wouldn't want to have groceries the other people in town can't get."

"Like butter?"

"Yes, butter, and meat. I feel guilty sometimes about our dinner we get to eat on the base so I never eat the butter, and only the chicken meat. I wish I could fix you a supper as good as the dinner I get, but I can't."

The bus let the Grahams off a half mile from the house and they walked in silence there. J.T. knew she wanted to get home quickly to see if there was mail. If there wasn't a letter from Thad their talk about his day would be even more uncomfortable.

Grandma always left the mail on the kitchen table, unopened, and Alma went to it without speaking to her mother. There were six pieces which she went through quickly. Her shoulders slumped as she sat slowly into a chair. She went listlessly through the other letters again but opened none of them. J.T. and Grandma knew not to speak until Alma spoke to one of them. She signed deeply, then stacked the unopened mail at the farthest point away as if it were tainted and unwelcome.

"All right, put your lunch pail in the sink and come sit." J.T. wanted to ask if they could "sit" someplace else. Grandma had a large pot of some foul-smelling potion simmering on the stove. Probably collard greens, wild growing lamb's quarter, and who knows what else. If Thad were here he would say, out of earshot of course, "Get out the clothes pins, Grandma's cookin'." Mama ignored the smell and J.T.'s discomfort.

"Now then, why was Mr. Mac mad at you?"

"I swear I don't know, Mama. He was just fussin' at everything, talking to himself. Mad because the prisoners weren't there, I guess."

"No prisoners?"

"No, ma'am. Yesterday he kept yelling at them, said they were lazy, just kept yelling till they dropped their hoes and just sat down. Then Mr. Mac really yelled at them. Sergeant Preston had to calm him down, told him to go to the house and he'd handle it. So he left. Sergeant Preston gave us a thirty-minute break, and then we all went back to work. Today the prisoners didn't show up, so he took it out on me I guess."

"Did they take away his workers for good?"

"Don't think so, Mama, probably just wanted a day or two to cool off. I don't know. I hope not."

"Well, he should get Mexicans, not the trouble those Germans are, I'd imagine."

"Mama, the Mexicans only come up for the picking. The work's not steady enough the rest of the year. Farmers don't want to pay anybody for hoeing cotton anyways. Some of them just try to plow the weeds under, but that doesn't get the ones growing up in the cotton so there's got to be some hoeing done."

"Well, aren't you the farm expert now."

"Yes, ma'am.

"Mama?"

"Yes."

"Where's Mrs. McConnell? There's all these nice things in the house, you know, woman things, but I've never seen his wife."

"She's gone."

"Where?"

"Sister's, somewhere up by Amarillo."

"Why'd she leave?"

"If I tell you, I don't want you running to Beu and blab it all. None of his business. None of yours, really, but you work for the man and it's better I tell you than you askin' the wrong questions of Ed."

"What was her name, Mama?"

"Bessie—we called her Bess for short. I knew her and Ed years before they got married. She was a happy, fun-loving girl then, always laughing and carrying on. Her and Ed were married a long while, maybe fifteen years or so. Then one day she just up and left."

"Do you know why?"

"Yes, but it's of no matter to you."

"I'll just ask Farmer Mac, then."

"Don't you dare even think about it. I'll tell you, but so help me J.T. ..."

"I won't tell Beu, Mama! Did he hit her or something?"

"No, he just wore her down, wore her out I guess you'd say. All she did from morning to bedtime was work that farm. And that's okay, mind you, that's what farm women do, but ..."

"But what, Mama?"

"They never had any children, J.T. Bess wanted a family more than anything in the world, but it never happened. I think Ed wanted sons, too, least she said he did, but she never got pregnant. I told her to go see a doctor, but she said Ed wouldn't hear of it. So she just seemed to dry up, lose interest in everything, really. Pretty simple to figure out for someone on the outside like me. Work, work, no family to raise and love. Maybe not that simple if you're living it. So, like I said, one day just up and left. Left all her nice dishes, vases, pictures and things. Packed up her clothes and never came back. That's almost three years ago. Never asked for a penny from Ed, either, or so I'm told. Part of that farm is *hers*, but that's not for me to say."

"I think Mr. Mac would be a lot easier to get along with if she was still there."

"Likely. He's still hurtin', I 'spect."

"I sure hope we didn't lose the prisoners. They're good guys, especially Mr. Becker."

"I swear, J.T. If I hear you call them 'good' one more time ..."

"They're *good* to me, Mama. Mr. Becker and me talk all the time. He calls me "Kumpel," which means buddy. I'll bet he didn't do anything mean, just fought like he was told to."

"Once again, J.T. *Who* was he fighting?"

"He said the British, Mama. He said he never saw an American soldier till he was a prisoner. Some Australian soldiers captured him. Saw American planes and some tanks, he says."

"The British and Australians are on our side, J.T. Fighting them is the same as fighting America."

"I understand that, Mama. He's paying for it by being in this prison. He works all day for eighty cents. What good would it do for me not to talk to him? Just make the work day miserable for me, nothing to pass the time but work."

"That's what work is, J.T. It's putting in the time and getting paid a wage. You're not supposed to be entertained."

"I don't see what the harm is, Mama. He don't mean hurt to me. He's a father, not a monster." J.T.'s eyes began to tear. Alma did not continue the exchange. With "He's a father" came the look of sadness she'd seen before. J.T. couldn't remember his father, taken by the Woodie Guthrie disease years before, a mythical presence talked about by his older siblings but just a half dozen washed-out photos to the boy. Alma had never known how to address the empty spot. Her attempts had been disasters. She had asked a son-in-law to have a "birds and bees" talk with J.T., but it had been met with J.T.'s snickering as the poor man searched for names for the body parts that he thought Alma would find acceptable. A car man, he had chosen automobile metaphors to make his points. Something about warming up the engine, then putting it in gear. J.T. couldn't remember it all, his concentration destroyed at that point, as had been the lesson.

A planned summer with her sister Florence and the male influence of her brother-in-law had proven to be equally unproductive, as well as lacking the humor of the sex lecture. Alma's brother-in-law would have been a natural for silent movie westerns. At home he seldom spoke in excess of a few dozen words a day, most of the one syllable variety with a nonexistent sense of timing. Though he was now a pump station troubleshooter for Conoco Oil, twenty-five years before he had been the best bronc buster in East Texas. A diminutive well-muscled man, he still wore a cowboy hat and boots three hundred fifty-six days a year. His boys grown and married, he had nothing to offer J.T. except silence and a boot in the rear if he got out of line, much the same contribution he had made to the raising of his own two sons. After two weeks, J.T. asked to come home.

In junior high, J.T. had developed an admiration for his gym teacher. Alma had been grateful for the man's mentoring and the positive things he had to say about her son. It had lasted a year. The "coach" had moved on, finally realizing his goal of a high school coaching position that took him to a town several hundred miles away.

Alma gave little thought to marrying again, consumed with sole support of a family and a troublesome mother. Would any man have wanted to take on a woman with six children, a needy mother, damaged legs, who could bring no financial contribution to the union? She thought not.

"It doesn't matter, Mama. Otto, Mr. Becker, hasn't been at work for a week. Sergeant Preston said he "had a little accident" and laughed, so I don't know what that means."

"You call him *Mr.* Becker?"

"Yes, Ma'am."

"He's a German prisoner, J.T."

"You never said that made any difference."

Alma Graham was hoisted with her own petard of manners here and she knew it.

"Well, you wouldn't have to call him anything if you didn't talk to him."

"Mama …"

"What do you talk about?"

"Everything—Otto knows about most everything. He has a whole bunch of education and taught in this famous German school, and sometimes he's funny, too."

"Why don't you just talk to the guard? He's one of our Army boys, isn't he?" J.T. sat back in his chair and surrendered with is body, unwilling to pursue it further.

"Can I go now, Mama?" Alma felt her inadequacy. There was no point in putting a nagging hurt on him any longer. The five children before him had turned out all right. *You'd think I'd just be able to relax and enjoy this one.*

"Yes, you can go now. And J.T. …"

"Yes, Mama?"

"I love you, Son."

"I love you too, Mama."

Chapter 17

OTTO CHOSE NOT TO take advantage of the Sunday outdoors. He didn't want to upset the mood of the camp, a depressed atmosphere that he might make volatile again. Klaus, who had avoided him for several days, appeared to be working on his "plan." He sat with von Hoffmann and two of the SS man's cronies at the football game in full swing on the dirt sweep. The field had been marked today with some white powder and some of the prisoners had commandeered material to make nets for the goals. The competition was loud, if not accomplished. He had heard a guard tell them that this was the last time he would return the ball if they kicked it over the fence once again. Otto wondered why the guards didn't open the gate and let a prisoner fetch it. No one would be foolish enough to chase the ball, then make a fatal dash for freedom.

Klaus had engaged von Hoffmann in continuous dialogue for fifteen minutes. What conversational subject they had in common he couldn't imagine. *Hoffy, old boy, I know you're just a misunderstood murderer who really has everyone's best interests at heart. Can we just be friends, until I kill you?*

Otto tired of standing at the door watching and went inside and sat on his bunk. He still felt some effects of the beating but it was no worse than Bir el Gubi where he had been felled by the concussion from an exploding shell. On that occasion, he had returned to full combat in three days. Too many thoughts free-floating in his mind now, he must focus, regain control of the here and now, survive.

He realized that no one had received the stockade for the barracks riot, including himself. Colonel Payne had but three punishments: the stockade for the most serious, loss of canteen privileges, and docking their pay chits. Canteen privileges were a hollow threat, the punished prisoner simply giving his money to a friend to buy for him. Loss of pay hurt more, of course. Otto had spent three days in the stockade for his "Crazy Otto" episode. Bread and water was bothersome but *white* bread and water could take you to the brink. Seven prisoners hung for killing a man in another camp *had* made an impression. He had some doubts about the story but, true or not, Klaus was right, trading his life for von Hoffmann's was not a good option. And if he or Klaus successfully accomplished the feat of eliminating von Hoffmann, then what? Two privates certainly weren't going to suddenly be in charge of the Camp 67 prisoners. What outcome then? A huggy, kissy population overflowing with good will? That was not likely. These men were hardened, tough soldiers who, unlike Otto, would simply follow *whomever* was in command. A return to Captain Müeller's more benevolent direction would be a relief for all except the Nazis, left without their Obersturmführer. He and Klaus had never been able to say for certain who was a Nazi or Gestapo, but they were sure von Hoffmann was the only SS member on board. Otto had always separated them in his mind by clothing: the Gestapo wore civilian clothes, leather overcoats, and hats; the SS usually appeared in their distinctive uniform. The Gestapo were the State Secret Political Police, not a large numbered force, having forty-six thousand men at their peak. The Gestapo cracked down on internal dissention, were in charge of rounding up the Jews, gypsies, homosexuals, traitors, and spies. Being small in number, given the breadth of the German-occupied territories, they primarily relied upon denunciations for their arrests. They did not have to show cause nor were few they arrested ever given trial. The myth of the Gestapo being everywhere was that, a myth. They could not keep up with the denunciations by "good German citizens" or collaborators. The arrest term used by the Gestapo was, "You are being taken into 'protective custody.'" Given the Gestapo's absolute impunity from accountability, many times they did not bother with an arrest and simply shot the "suspect" on the spot.

That they were involved with the SS in mass murder was beyond doubt. Hermann Göering founded the Gestapo but Heinrich Himmler was able to wrest control from Göering; by doing so, he headed both the SS and the Gestapo.

The SS, which stood for Schutzstaffel, literal meaning *protective squadron,* was an elite command whose original purpose, under Nazism, was to protect Hitler. Himmler grew it into a parallel army numbering over eight hundred thousand, and at this stage of the war one that was becoming dominant over the regular German Army. Among their tasks was addressing the "Jewish Question." Adolf Eichmann headed the SS branch which sought the answer. The SS was to have been made up of pure Aryan Germans, requiring proof of superior racial purity with no Jewish ancestors. Their fierce loyalty to Hitler and the Nazi cause made them a cult to rival any of periods before or after. The SS answered directly to Hitler, though Himmler was titular head and the director of the day-to-day operations.

Before Camp 67, Otto had little contact with either of the dreaded services. Rommel protected his men from any outside threat or influence that might distract from their job of fighting. The school where Otto had taught had three teachers removed by the Gestapo, three of their best, but unfortunately Jewish. The curriculum had been altered somewhat to reflect some of the history revisions and Nazi propaganda demanded by the Reich, but less so than other schools because of its elite and long-standing reputation, and more practically, the fact that the sons of many of the favored civilian gentility and high-ranked German military officers attended there. Otto's curriculum as a language teacher was affected almost not at all. Young German men needed to learn the languages of countries already conquered, or soon to be, if they were to properly vanquish, occupy, loot and then transform the population into consequential Nazis.

Men began to filter in twos and threes into the barracks and congregate around the water casks, drinking and discussing the football match which, apparently, had ended shortly before. Otto buried his face in a book and did not make eye contact with any of his fellow prisoners. He wished for a quick passage of the rest of the afternoon, then the fitful night of sleep. Tomorrow he would return to work.

Chapter 18

THERE WAS SOME DISAPPOINTMENT for Otto as he prepared to fall out for the morning inspection by Obersturmführer Werner von Hoffmann. Not a disappointment in the inspection—he looked forward to that—but in the doctor's order to serve two more days of light-duty barracks cleanup. He needed to get back to the farm. There he must find or fashion some weapon that he would surely need as long as von Hoffmann was in charge. He could not risk taking on another attack unarmed.

The Texas weather had taken one of its sudden turns, yesterday warm and humid, today cloudy with a welcome early morning coolness. The canteen corporal who sold him cigarettes yesterday had said rain was imminent. He was a farm boy, he had said, and a good farmer could smell rain up to twenty-four hours before it appeared. Otto smelled nothing but the cured ham and beef jerky that hung in strips from an upside-down Lazy Susan. He knew one thing: there was no beer in the building. A farmer might smell rain but a German could smell beer through concrete and steel walls.

Von Hoffmann's hobnailed boots resonated off the concrete assembly slab. It was a chilling sound, sharp, clinging to the ear seconds after its issue, alien to the norm like the little man whose pacing created it. Von Hoffmann seemed even more arrogant than before Otto's beating. He pranced down each line of prisoners, rocking to his tiptoes before each soldier who stood, frozen at attention, eyes forward. His dealing with

Otto's insolence had made the point, if it ever needed to be made, that the SS lieutenant was firmly in charge.

Private Otto Becker stood in the rear line of soldiers. Klaus had positioned himself three lines away and had made no contact as they fell in. Otto glanced at von Hoffmann just soldiers away, eager, he was sure, to address his former nemesis. Von Hoffmann stopped before him and looked up into his face, the Obersturmführer's lip curled in contempt. He stepped back in astonishment. Around Otto Becker's neck the Knight's Cross of the Iron Cross hung by a black-and-white ribbon.

"Where did you get that?"

"From Field Marshal Erwin Rommel, June 23, 1942, in Tobruk."

"You're lying, lying; you took it off a dead soldier. You're no hero!"

"Check the records with your superb Berlin contacts you keep telling us about."

"I will check NOTHING! Give me that!" Von Hoffmann reached for the medal only to have Becker grab his arm in a viselike grip and hold it.

"I see, I see. It appears you did not learn your lesson the last time. *Crazy* Otto. You are indeed crazy!"

"All events are learning experiences. Yes, I learned a great deal. I will say this (shouts loudly) to you and to the cowards who attack sleeping men. Try again and see if I earned this medal or stole it!" He released von Hoffmann's wrist. The Obersturmführer stomped away into the officer's barracks without another word. The guards had observed the confrontation and quickly moved in.

"All right, that's it. Form your working details, base details to the left, farm details to the right!"

The prisoners moved slowly to their designated spots, mumbling among themselves and glancing at the officer's barracks might von Hoffmann come storming out. They averted Otto's eyes, still wide and flaming, moving away from the spot where he stood, their movement either in fear of him or for him. Surely, this time, he had confirmed his death sentence.

My boot camp sergeant would be proud of me, Otto thought as he sat on his bunk. *I spread out the troops this morning, so scattered it would have taken ten grenades to get us.* He was now Camp 67's leper. No one wanted to be in the blood spatter zone. Time for Otto to say good-bye to West Texas? On his own terms or others? He'd have to see how things played out in the next days, see what Klaus had in mind, keep rolling the dice like he had so many times in North Africa, not afraid to die which had translated into not the time to die. So many close encounters, so many dead comrades. Somehow he'd delayed the event a bit. He had once quoted Kafka to Klaus when they were discussing the selection process of death in the battlefield. One man dies, another lives. Why? Kafka had said, "There is no clear answer to life, just what you come up with." Klaus had answered, "Kafka was a Jew." "Ah, Klaus," he had replied, "to think so *deeply* must be liberating indeed. So, Herr Kafka, the Jew, I have come up with *irony* as my answer. Yes, *irony,* sir! Our allotted time filled with random ironies. Young Bach dies, Becker lives. That's all the meaning there is."

The immediate task for Otto was to find a better hiding place for his medal. He had hidden it in his boot and the lining of his bag during his ship and train journeys. An Iron Cross would be a sweet score for the American soldier souvenir collectors and his fellow Germans who stole and sold any piece of German gear they could obtain. At Camp 67 the selling of lesser medals, pins, and decorated belt buckles was common. In fact a German prisoner, Corporal Klein, had become the successful middle man for the prisoners and a guard who dealt with off-base souvenir collectors. Buttons were ripped from uniforms, as well as sleeve insignias. American money was valued by those who sought to have purchases made for them in town or to squirrel away for future escape attempts. One by one, Otto had seen the distinctive billed cap of the Afrika Korps disappear from daily view. Other than medals such as Otto's, and certain campaign medals, it was the most desired and salable item.

Otto, alone in the barracks, returned the medal to his mattress. He had made a slit underneath the heavy bottom seam large enough to slide it back into the cotton stuffing. Now that others knew he had it, it would not be safe anywhere. Give it to a friend to hide? Maybe Wagner. No one would dare go near the gear of the massive felon. He thought of Kumpel, but he wasn't at all sure the boy's mother would allow him to keep a medal for a German soldier. It was a dilemma that helped take his mind off the more serious issues he faced. In reality, the medal was not important in the long term.

Otto thought of the Iron Cross story his father had told him. His father had said Adolph Hitler was a much decorated soldier in World War I. He had been wounded twice and blinded by gas. He had voluntarily returned to the front lines, where several times over four years he had been given combat honors. Among his medals was the Iron Cross for bravery in battle, an award seldom given to a foot soldier in those days. Otto's father told him the story, not because he was an admirer or follower of Hitler, quite the opposite. His father had served as a combat surgeon in the war and had taken basic training with a man who later led one of the units in which Hitler served. His friend was the officer who recommended Corporal Hitler for the Iron Cross. The officer was a JEW! Dr. Becker had said, "You notice that fact has never been made public!" *Ahh, irony indeed.*

That evening Klaus nodded to Otto indicating he should follow him into the latrine. Klaus put his back to the doors so no one could enter. He spoke quietly through tense lips and gritted teeth.

"Your stupid ego! Now they have another reason to kill you. Your medal is worth a month of our pay. Why can't you keep your mouth shut and give me some time? No, you must play the hero, the man who can stand up to the SS! You're going to be buried in this God-forsaken prairie. Stupid! Stupid!

"That's enough. Don't talk to me that way again, *ever!* I'm tired of you treating me like a schoolboy. Stay away from me! Make your plan. I will make mine. I think you will find kissing an SS man's ass is a very slow way to kill him, it takes quite a pucker.

"Now get out of my way."

Chapter 19

WITH TWO EXTRA DAYS on his hands Otto filled them by sitting on his hidden medal like a nesting bird on her eggs. Then two coming visits were posted of off-base individuals who might help him in the area more important to him than his safety, the medal, or his physical condition: the unexplained lack of communication from his wife and son. Otto had written a letter every week either to his Dresden address, his parents, or his wife's family in Berlin. It made no sense that he had gotten no answer from any of them. Mail came in every day. Some prisoners had received more than one letter, some pictures and small trinket gifts. He wasn't alone in the dearth of mail, but in his unscientific survey it seemed he was the only married one with parents, in-laws, and a school whose headmaster had even written him while he was in North Africa. The Red Cross and a Catholic priest would be available today and he would see both.

Otto was escorted to the base chapel to meet the priest. It was his first time, other than the hospital, to see any of the buildings on the base or to walk on the grounds, given his daily exit and return to the base both being by truck. Otto went in; the guard stayed outside the door. Otto assumed there was no back exit and if there was no one seemed worried. In the four months he had been at Camp 67 he had noticed the security, if it had not relaxed, had at least exhaled and no longer seemed to worry about escapes. Except for Crazy Otto there had not been a disturbance of that nature, and it was reflected in the attitude of the guards who had in many cases developed rapport if not friendship with some of the POWs.

The base builders had done a commendable job on the chapel. Perhaps the town, which forbade alcohol, had insisted on it. The lighting was low key, almost somber; the interior, dark woods with wooden, cushioned pews. The pulpit was simple, a large cross set above and behind a beautiful oak lectern. A choir chancel was on its right with twenty to thirty chairs and six other chairs had been placed in front of a velvet maroon drop that hung like an opera curtain behind the entire pulpit stage. It was meant to be nondenominational and was.

A small table had been placed between the front pew and the pulpit. The priest stood in front of a chair on one side and he motioned Otto to the other. The priest was a ruddy, round-faced man, veins and red blotches dominated a cleric face of almost unreal perfection.

"How do you do, son? I'm Father Murphy."

"Private Becker, sir, Father."

"Good to meet someone who doesn't laugh at the Father Murphy Irish priest thing the first time they hear it."

"Pardon?"

"I'm a walking cliché, Private Becker, Irish priest named Murphy."

"Well, if you'd said Father Barry Fitzgerald I might have giggled a bit. I have seen *that* American movie."

"Yes, marvelous actor. Defined Irish priests forever. Is Becker a common name, as well? In Germany, I mean."

"Well, not uncommon, but we have our Smiths and Joneses, too. Probably Müller and Schmidt if I had to hazard a guess as the two most prevalent."

"When they told me I wouldn't need an interpreter I assumed you would speak English, but you are exceptional."

"I was a teacher of language, Father. English and French for the most part, but I speak Spanish also. That career was before I became a soldier who managed to get himself captured."

"Have you come for confession, Private Becker?"

"No, Father, I'm not even a Catholic. The reason I came is not really religious; though I consider myself a believer, I've never been a religious person, one who practiced his faith. My wife and I did on occasion attend the Frauenkirche, Church of Our Lady in Dresden. If you've never seen it, it's one of the most beautiful churches in Europe. To be honest, we attended as an attempt to be good parents. We felt it was only fair that our son be exposed to religion of some sort so that at some time he would have a point of reference when it came time to make a decision of belief for himself. It's because of my wife and son that I've come to see you today. You see, I haven't heard from her or any of my relatives for almost half a year. Something has to be terribly wrong."

"Private, this is a better question for the Red Cross, but it's one I get asked often by prisoners. I don't have the connections or access to information of this sort. When I pass the question on to persons who work in these areas they simply tell me 'there's a war on.' Many American relatives are in the same situation as you, having not heard from a son or husband in months—it's a war and nothing is the same. Mail is important to the armies of both sides, but it is not at the top of their priorities."

"I know this isn't your job, Father, but I've written down all my information, names, addresses, at least the last addresses I had. I understand telephone numbers are useless, since calls into Germany must have military clearance. I want to give you this, and if at any time you come across someone who *does* have some sort of link to Dresden citizens, names of civilians killed or injured, anything, maybe you could ask about my wife and son. That's all I'm asking."

"I'll take your information, Private Becker, but you need to know I've never run into such a person yet and the odds are not good I will."

"I understand."

"One thing I could ask other clerics and that is, are there church connections between any American churches and those in Germany? Maybe the church you mentioned could be contacted."

"I would be very grateful."

"I should be back in a month. I'll contact you again then. I rotate between prison camps. The priest, minister, preacher is different each week here. Prisoner attendance has been very poor at Camp 67. Of course, this is a small camp. Perhaps it is a function of despair brought on by their imprisonment. I don't know."

"I think attendance is discouraged here."

"By whom?"

"Obersturmführer von Hoffmann. He's our happy little SS midget. Those who attend are labeled 'reactionaries.' Another factor is the number of young soldiers we have here. They came up through the Hitler Youth. Their God is Adolph Hitler."

"You're very brave, or foolish, to be so candid, Private Becker."

"They don't intimidate me. If I wished to attend church, I would do so."

"And you don't?"

"No."

"Why?"

"As you know, religion was not banned by the Nazi government and we even had chaplains in our military units, but there was always pressure from the Nazis in the battalions to not attend. I suspect, ultimately, religion will be abolished in Germany. I attended, on occasion, in the Afrika Korps simply to show I would not be cowed, rather than a religious interest."

"You have no interest in God, Private Becker?"

"God is far away from me now, Father."

"And who moved?"

Otto didn't answer.

"God is a rock who won't move, Private Becker. He'll be there when you're ready to come back. Will you come to a service soon, my son? Even if it is to defy those who would have you deny God?"

"I will."

"We leave literature and Bibles in the barracks. Have you seen them?"

"Yes, but I've never seen anyone reading them."

"Some are in German."

"I'm reading a book now that is biblical in some ways, called *The Grapes of Wrath*."

"Of course, Revelation 14:19–20. 'And the angel thrust in his sickle into the earth, and cast it into the great winepress of the wrath of God. And the winepress was trodden without the city, and blood came out of the winepress, even unto the horse bridles, by the space of a thousand and six furlongs. And in the eyes of the hungry, there is a growing wrath. In the souls of the people the grapes of wrath are filling and growing heavy from the vintage.'"

"Very impressive to have that right on the tip of your tongue, Father."

"I confess I just did a sermon on that passage just a week ago. Yes, most people believe the book title comes from our 'Battle Hymn of the Republic': 'He is trampling out the vintage where the grapes of wrath are stored.' But you can see it goes back well before the song."

"I see that."

"Do you serve a sacrament at your services, Father?"

"Yes."

"Is it real wine? If it is, I'll be there."

"You'll have to come and find out. We're working, actually the protestant ministers more than me, to allow prisoners to be transported into town for services on Sunday. We can't insist, just suggest, but that might be good. We're all God's children."

"But we're the wicked children here. I don't think the townspeople would want us around, even on a Sunday morning in church. Although from my experience, the townspeople were friendly when I visited them."

"You—visited?"

"Long story, Father. You find my wife and son, and I'll tell you my Crazy Otto adventure. You'll get it before the novel and the movie based on the novel."

"I think you are having fun with me now, Private Becker. Unless there's something else, I must conclude our meeting. Know that I will pray for you and your family. I will also talk to Colonel Payne about prisoners being discouraged from church services by this officer. It has been good talking to you I always learn from my discussions with German prisoners, and many times it gives me hope to go along with my faith. Now I must get back to Camp McLean. I have a marriage to perform today."

"Who's getting married, a guard?"

"No, a prisoner."

"A prisoner? How could that be?"

"Simple, actually. The camp commander and I meet with the prisoner. He makes his vows witnessed by the two of us, then signs some papers. Those papers are sent back to a magistrate in Germany who performs the ceremony with the wife to be. She then signs the papers and under German law they are officially married."

"You mean a POW can get married by mail and I can't even get a letter from my wife? Ridiculous!"

"I'm sorry about you not being able to contact your wife, but ..."

"Could you send along a request about my family when you mail the marriage papers back?"

"That's an idea. I *will* try that."

"Thank you, Father Murphy. I felt better after our talk, but now I just feel frustrated again."

"I will pray for you, Private Becker."

Chapter 20

GENEVA CONVENTION 1929
Prisoners of war may be interned in a town, fortress, or other place and may not go beyond fixed limits.

Prisoners of war may employ as workmen who are physically fit, other than officers and persons of equivalent statue.

Prisoners of war are entitled to respect for their persons and honour.

No prisoner of war shall be pressured to declare other than his true name, rank, or his regimental number.

Prisoners of war will be lodged in buildings or barracks affording all guarantees of health and hygiene. Quarters must be protected from dampness and sufficiently heated and lighted.

Prisoners of war must be given food rations equal in quantity and quality to that of troops at the base camps where they are held captive.

Prisoners of war shall not be forced to do unhealthy or dangerous work. Marches on foot shall not exceed twenty kilometers.

Seven of the 97 articles of the Geneva Convention.

The Red Cross workers met with prisoners in the mess hall. Three women sat at tables sufficiently separated to allow that the conversations might not be overheard. An armed guard stood at the door, another sorted out the order of the queue waiting for entrance to the building. The Red Cross business, unlike the priest's, was brisk.

Otto approached the only table unoccupied by a POW. The woman who greeted him was middle thirties, Otto estimated, dressed conservatively, her hair pulled back in a bun, and wearing no makeup. Best not get the prisoners excited, Otto had imagined her instructions to be. Her only jewelry was a gold wedding band. Otto had seen some female Red Cross workers as they boarded the train to Texas, passing out shaving gear and cigarettes and sometimes homemade sweets. He had never been this close. Otto felt a stirring, followed by a sense of shame that he had been so moved. Here to seek help finding his family and attracted to the woman he hoped would assist him.

"*Guten Nachmittag, Gefreiter Becker. Wie Kann ich ihnen helfen?*"

"I speak English."

"Oh good, as you can tell my German is 'passable,' as I am told. Barely, I would imagine."

"You did fine."

"You are Private Otto Franz Becker?"

"Yes."

"I'm Mary Lindsey. Now, may I see your Soldbuch and your Erkennungsmarke?"

Otto took out his identity booklet, a soiled, wrinkled, document that had been with him for four years. The Soldbuch contained his name, picture (almost unintelligible), medical history, and his battalion, now as obsolete as the picture of a younger man smiling into the camera. He bent over the table to allow her to look at his identity tags.

"Could you take them off, please?" Otto did so. "Looks like everything matches."

"Yes. No one in this camp would pretend to be me. Would you like to speak German, for the practice?"

"No, thank you."

"French? Spanish?"

"I don't speak either," she said in a businesslike voice.

"I probably don't either, it's been so long. Too long to remember how to do a lot of things," he found himself saying. *Stupid Dummkopf!* Mary Lindsey appeared to not take note.

"I have a question to ask you first. Then I will try to answer yours. I have your camp records here. I understand you were hospitalized, just recently it seems, with a number of injuries. Can you tell me about that?"

"If you have my records you'll see I already talked to an investigator about that. My answers haven't changed."

"Private Becker, if someone has injured you, I can help. We've been able to transfer people involved in these altercations to other camps for their safety or punishment for their involvement. Would you like to be transferred?"

"It's a thought, but I think not at this point. There are some lovely people here I'd miss, and to whom I'm in debt. And to leave without paying one's debts is not good form, I would think."

"Then you don't want to talk about, let's see here, 'falling out of your bunk.'"

"I don't want to be reminded of my clumsiness."

"I see. The form you filled out says you wish help in making contact with your family in Germany. We do a lot of that."

Otto repeated the absence of mail, the mail others received, and his intense worry that something has happened to his loved ones in Germany.

"It does seem odd you would not have heard from at least one of the three families. I'll check into it as soon as I return to our headquarters."

"And that is?"

"Dallas. I'll also check with Camp Hearne."

"How could they help? Camp Hearne is a POW camp?"

"Yes, a large one, located southeast of here. They are the distribution point for all prisoner mail in the state."

"Verdammt, verdammt, verdammt."

"Private Becker, don't jump to conclusions. I'll look into it, and remember I will be trying to make contacts for you in both Dresden and Berlin."

"And Frankfurt, that's where my parents now live, or lived."

"Yes, Frankfurt."

Otto seethed inside. *This must be the answer. Von Hoffmann's 'friends' at Hearne and those who handle mail at Camp 67 **must** be the answer. There is no other, except for the unthinkable.*

"Private Becker ..." Otto had gripped the table's edge and was clearly agitated. "Private Becker, I said we'll look into it! Now, do you have any other questions, requests, or complaints?"

Otto did not answer. He tried to compose himself and channel the anger to the inside. This woman had nothing to do with his problem. She and her agency alone could make contact with a counterpart in his country who could then pursue information about his wife and child. Even the mighty Allied armies did not possess that access.

"Requests, complaints, Private Becker?"

"Yes, where's the beer?" Otto said aggressively. "And don't tell me this is a *dry* county. Your prohibition didn't work in the '20s, I don't think it would work now. I know there is beer because the guards make light of my search for it, 'rub it in,' I think Americans say."

"I have to take the official line, Private Becker. I know the colonel has been working on the question. Beer is available to prisoners at other camps, I do know that, but the Red Cross doesn't think it's proper for them to lobby for it here."

"We will have to brew our own hooch, as some call it. So far the attempts have been undrinkable at best. They've tried potatoes, they've tried fruit. Germans need their beer, Frau Lindsey."

"I'll pretend I didn't hear about your moonshine stills. Now, some of your comrades have requested music and a record player. We're going to be able to do that for the camp. What are your music preferences?"

"Symphonic, operatic, the great German composers."

"All right, but you have a number of younger prisoners here and many not as educated as you or who have your musical tastes."

"Let them listen to 'Mares Eat Oats,' or Gerhardt can sing them, 'You Are My Sunshine.'"

"I'll note your request, the latter part I will describe as jest."

"I couldn't be more serious, Frau Lindsey."

She moved on. "Now, the availability of literature in German has improved, hasn't it? We have sent out magazines and a few books. Have you seen them?"

"Yes, I've seen them around."

"But reading English is no problem for you, correct? You've likely had reading material all along. Private Becker, I've been wondering, and you certainly don't have to answer this, but I'm curious why an educated man who speaks three languages is still a private."

Otto grinned. "No offense, Frau Lindsey. Other than being a smartass and offending most officers I've served under, it's by request, mine. On occasion I've been offered promotions. I've declined."

"And they didn't just promote you anyway?"

"I think, Frau Lindsey, that soldiers who are willing to fight, up close, and very well, if I may, how do you say it, toot my own whistle ..."

"Horn."

"Yes, you're right. Horn. Anyway, a soldier of my caliber is more difficult to come by than a worthless officer. There—toot, toot!"

"Commendable, I'm sure. But I doubt you'll find many foot soldiers who share your feelings. Anything else?"

"I am not a complainer. I think you Americans are stupid for treating us, feeding us as you do. I don't complain. The accommodations here are luxury compared to North Africa."

"Some say the barracks are too hot at night."

"You should laugh in their faces if they make such complaints. Camp 67 is a seaside resort compared to where we came from. This treatment you give us has made some of the men soft. They forget very quickly."

"Well, I think Colonel Payne agrees with you. We passed on a prisoner request for fans in the barracks and he seemed to think that was quite funny. My last question. Have you had tornado drills on how to protect yourself if one hits? You are in cyclone alley, you know."

"Tornado drills! That's even better than fans, madam. I helped build these barracks. If a tornado hits us, you'll find our asses in Oklahoma. The farmer's chicken house is more secure, better built. You think they care if a bunch of Germans become airborne?"

"Thank you. I take it our pursuing tornado drills is a waste of our time."

"The breath you just spent on it is a waste."

Frau Lindsey paused, giving Becker time to continue if he wished. She would question no more. Though Otto had been a refreshing change from the usual interviews, she knew other POWs were waiting.

"Private Becker, it was good talking to you. If I find out any information about your family, I will call Camp 67 and have it passed on to you immediately."

"I would be forever indebted, Frau Lindsey." By habit or desire, he didn't know which, he extended his hand. She shook it briefly. The touch of a woman felt good, fleeting or not.

Chapter 21

EVERYTHING HAD CHANGED AFTER the Iron Cross incident. His fellow prisoners treated Otto with a newfound respect, the medal and the physical challenge to von Hoffmann became the defining Becker characteristic for them. "Crazy Otto" had become memory rather than a title. Otto's explanation of that incident was credible now. The new respect with which his peers held him had not changed his status of dead man walking. Only Hans and Wagner dared to talk to him at any length around the barracks compound. His farm coworkers, safely out of the sight and sound of the SS and Nazi elements, carried on as before. Otto had been their leader and de facto "boss" before, so hero admiration only solidified it.

This was Otto's first day back at work. The nine men and J.T. had been divided into three work groups with different tasks. They were not in sight of each other so Sergeant Preston split the difference, which just happened to be a shade tree in back of the barn. He sat upon his perch reading a copy of a Zane Grey western, his rifle slung by strap on a nail hammered into the chair's arm expressly for that purpose. It was dull duty beyond belief but preferable to the guard towers or prisoner escort details, and only slightly more dangerous than swabbing the latrine. Here he was the CO, the badass, the King.

J.T. had attached himself to Otto's group. Sergeant Preston had waved him on, knowing he would work his way to Otto's side eventually anyway. Preston made a mental note to talk to the boy about getting attached to a man who might be transferred to another farm or to on-base duty. He hesitated to tell him of the rumor that said the detail Becker was most likely to join was those whose bodies had assumed room temperature. J.T. had peppered Otto with a week of questions he had saved up. Otto's group was repairing thirty feet of fence that Farmer McConnell's bull had destroyed. The bull had been in one field, the heifers in heat in another, and the fence in between. Otto had told Sergeant Preston that the prisoners would fix the fence but the army could deal with the bull.

"So, Kumpel, did you find Dresden, Germany, and North Africa on the map as I told you?"

"Yes, sir, but I had to get the custodian to let me into the geography room at school. We don't have any maps at home."

"You should get one, Kumpel. Hang it on your wall next to your Betty Grable picture and then you could follow the war in Europe, country by country, as well as your brother's in Asia."

"I don't have a room, Mr. Becker, and if I put up a picture of Betty Grable anywhere it would last about ten seconds."

"No room? Where do you sleep?"

"On the couch. In our other house my brother and me shared a room. That was good."

"Buy the map anyway, Kumpel, it will be educational."

"I need to buy my school clothes for next year with my wages. Then after that, my Charles Atlas course."

"You're still planning on paying a man to give you some muscles, huh. Kumpel, you are building your muscles every day you work here. I can see you getting bigger and stronger all the time."

"Really?"

"Absolutely. A few more months and Charles Atlas will be taking your course, *Feeding Pigs to Build the Perfect Body*."

"That's funny."

"Do you like school, Kumpel?"

"It's okay. Most of the good men teachers my brother and sister had are off in the service. Just the old ones or ones that are 4F are there now, lots more women teachers. But it's okay. The coaches aren't very good, some people coaching that didn't even play the sport. But that's war, I guess. That's the way people explain it, anyway. Can you tell me more about the war you were in, Mr. Becker? I wish there wasn't a war, but war stories are exciting."

"It's not glamorous like the movies and books make it, Kumpel. It's sordid, to tell you the truth."

"Sordid, what's that?"

"Filthy, foul, despicable, vicious, all the negative adjectives you learned in your classes."

"Were you in the artillery, Mr. Becker, or the army?"

Otto smiled. "I was in the 115 Rifle Regiment, 15th Panzer Division. Infantry that supports the tanks and artillery. That's what panzer means, loosely, tanks and artillery."

"You were captured in Africa, right? Like Tarzan Africa, jungle and elephants and such?"

"No, more Arabian Nights Africa. No trees to swing from where we were. Just desert."

"Wow!"

Otto saw the look of awe and admiration on J.T.'s face. "Kumpel, you're a foolish boy, admiring men like me. The enemy cannot be admired or be a hero for you. I've tried to tell you this before. There are plenty of men for you to admire: Americans, General Eisenhower or General Patton, your brother. Your brother should be the one you look up to, not a POW, a soldier who fought and killed allies of your country. It's *wrong*, Kumpel. You are a fine boy and I enjoy talking to you, but never make more of me than I am. The world can't be full of friends. There *must* be enemies or we have no perspective. Did you study history?"

"Yes, sir."

"Did you ever read and wonder why there is always a war? You say why can't everyone just be friends? Because it runs against human nature, the male half, at least. They need war to prove themselves men. Now that I've been to war I know it proves nothing. You will be a man by taking care of your family, raising your children, providing for their needs. That's the kind of man I'd like to be again, that's the man you need to be."

"I'm going to be a Marine like my brother."

"You didn't hear a word I said, did you? You want to hear war stories."

"When do you think the war will be over, Mr. Becker? And what if Germany loses?"

"I'd like to see it end. I won't lie, I hope we win but I think not. Our best hope would be to seek a truce, withdraw from our conquered territories and rebuild our country."

"Truce, like a surrender?"

"A surrender of sorts, prevent the invasion of our country. We fear an invasion by the Russians would doom us. The Americans could be negotiated with; your Red Cross is an indication of that to me. I'm talking in riddles to you, aren't I? You're too young to understand war, too uneducated to know the consequences of losing one. Let's talk about something else."

"Well, okay. I been thinking while you were gone about some stuff. First is that funny thing you wear around your neck. It looks a little like my brother's dog tags he showed me when he was home on leave."

"This?" Otto pulled the metal tag out from his shirt. "This is our identification tag. It has information about the soldier wearing it. It's two parts, see, both have the same information. They can be separated by bending them back and forwards. If a German soldier is killed, they take the lower half for recordkeeping and leave the other half on the dead body. Your soldiers wear two tags for the same purpose."

"Wow, looks like it would break."

"No, it's very strong. Zinc maybe, I'm not sure. Next question? It's like I'm being interviewed today, Herr Kumpel. Are you secretly a reporter or a spy, seeking information?"

"I think I'd make a better spy. I don't write very good."

"Yes, not encouraging when my grammar is better than yours."

"Crazy Otto."

"That's your question?"

"You said you'd tell me someday, Mr. Becker."

"All right, at lunch, or dinner as you call it, we'll find a nice cool spot and I'll tell you while we eat."

"I can hardly wait to tell Beu!"

"Perhaps this will be good. You won't think so highly of me when you hear how I got the title. After I tell you, I will teach you the German word 'Dummkopf.' Then you will be able to call me Private Dummkopf, the crazy prisoner of war."

Otto left the work party before the lunch call and made his way down to an area near the barn that served as a graveyard for every piece of abandoned machinery for the last fifty years. Rusted plows half-buried in drifting sand; a tractor so beaten by weather the brand name could no longer be read; pulleys; a rotary hoe; odd metal cans; a saw; the prize, a completely trashed '23 Packard, which had become a depository for metal pieces torn or removed from other metal pieces; buckets; and harnesses from a previous age of plowing. There was an ample number of items that would serve as a weapon, but he must find one that could be smuggled back on base, so size mattered. He dug as quietly as possible through the junk, hopefully before he was seen by McConnell or missed by Preston. Then he spotted a metal rod protruding from the ground. He pulled at it until the earth gave way. It was solid steel, eighteen inches long with a diameter of approximately an inch, he estimated. It gave no clue to its onetime function, but properly swung he believed it could do frightening damage. He held the bar in his hand and against his leg as he exited the junkyard and made his way to the assembly area for POW pickup at workday's end.

Otto and J.T. found their own shade tree at lunch. Sergeant Preston stared at them, apparently trying to decide if he should put an end to this association. Otto read the displeasure in his face but J.T. was oblivious. They were allowed their private site.

"I was working on another farm when the Crazy Otto incident occurred. Because of it, I was transferred to the McConnell farm."

"What did you do?"

"That's what I'm going to tell you, Kumpel. Don't interrupt.

"As I said, I had been on the farm, a nice man named Pace was the farmer, let's see, about two weeks. I had no problem with the work, no reason to try to escape. I knew escape was futile. But my thirst for a good cold beer got the best of me. I took a pair of the farmer's pants and a shirt off the clothesline of Frau Pace. I discarded my pants, put on his and buttoned the shirt over my POW shirt, walked off the farm and to a road nearby. I was picked up by a farmer going into town and we chatted like two old friends. I had a small amount of American money. I had exchanged my scrip, at three to one for the U.S. There is another private in the camp who works in the base laundry. He finds money quite frequently in the airmen's pockets before he washes them, enough to be a money changer in the camp. So there I am, a man in civilian clothes, who speaks the language and has enough money to buy a beer or, hopefully, two. When I get out on the street, I ask several people where is a *die Knoipe*. The first one I use the German word, the first crazy choice of the day. 'So, where are your bars?' I say. They all tell me this town is *dry*. Dry! Dry! What does that have to do with beer? They say no alcohol can be sold in this town, so it is *dry*. If they have beer, I guess it would be *wet*. I walk all over the town, looking in stores. Perhaps they didn't understand me. I went to a grocery store—nothing, just what you call soda pop. In one store I see these small wooden carvings of the State of Texas with a star at the location of 'Warner." So I buy it. Someday I will show my son where I was a prisoner. By then I am hungry so I go to a café. Should I buy food or continue to search for this *bootlegger* store where one man told me they sell alcohol? One man says a *bootlegger* will sell me the beer; two others don't know where the bootlegger store is located. I go to the café. I order a hamburger. They bring me water, which I needed, and my hamburger. Then I look up at the sign above the counter: ROOT BEER – 10¢ They lied! There IS beer! I have never heard of beer made from roots but it doesn't matter, beer is beer. They bring me this strange-looking beer, which is fizzling, *very* strange, but I drink.

"Have to spit it into my napkin. I finish my hamburger, I push the fizzling beer as far away as possible and concede defeat. I walked around town more, then I went to your courthouse and sat on a bench outside. I took my outer shirt off and sat on the bench with my POW shirt in full display. Two boys your age came along and asked me where I got the shirt. I said I captured a Nazi soldier and took it from him. They wanted to buy my shirt for a souvenir. I would have sold it, but there was no beer to spend the money on so I declined. I sat on the bench for a long time, admiring the ladies who walked or drove by. Then it was getting late and near suppertime. I was hungry again. If I got back to the camp quickly enough, I would be in time for the evening meal. There is a sheriff's office at your courthouse, so I went there and turned myself in. Instead of supper, I was thrown in the stockade for three days on bread and water. I made the mistake, I'd lost count of how many I'd made that day, made the mistake of telling the stockade guard the entire story. He said, 'Why didn't you steal a car while you were there and be "long gone,"' as he put it. Too stupid, too crazy I guess. So I did three days on bread and water thinking I would be served a hot meal, thought root beer was beer, became an escapee by record, a thief for stealing the clothes, and an instant legend because, of course, the guard told everyone on the base. People are still laughing at my *escape* to this day. The crazy Kraut, Otto Becker."

J.T. sat silently.

"No comment? Not even a laugh?"

"You should have tried some more of that root beer, Mr. Becker. It's really a good drink."

"Ahh, Kumpel, you *are* a delight!"

Otto had worked quickly to hide the steel rod. Using tape from a roll he had stolen in the hospital, he taped the metal piece to the inside of his left thigh. He could not walk normally but covered his limp by telling Sergeant Preston the injuries received in the barracks building were acting up once again. Sergeant Preston cared nothing about any pain Becker had. If he could get away with it, he'd add some of his own. Stinking Nazi killers, he'd like to line them all up and …

His thoughts were interrupted by J.T. saying goodbye. "See you tomorrow, Sergeant Preston," said the boy.

Yeah, kid, unfortunately another day babysitting Krauts, I'll be here, he thought. "See ya, J.T."

Phase one of getting the steel bar into the barracks had been successful. Phase two, the tough one, was the pat-down when they got off the truck and before entering the prison compound. MP Corporal Kincaid held the key there. Preston, Kincaid, and another sergeant named Scott did the prisoner search. Otto repeated to himself several times on the ride to the prison compound: *Kincaid **must** search me or I'll be in the stockade tomorrow.* Kincaid was a shy boy of nineteen who was good at his work, *except* the body search of prisoners. Kincaid recoiled at patting the inside legs of prisoners. They knew it and sometimes taunted him. Those who didn't speak English would moan if he put his hand past the ankle. "Oh, uhh, Corporal Kincaid." Those who had some command of English joined, "That feels so good, Corporal Kincaid—higher, higher, a little to the left." "Don't stop." "Gerhardt, is that you or are you smuggling in a bazooka?" Preston and Scott had no such reservations. If a prisoner made a sound while Preston was searching him, he got a fist to the testicles that bent him over for minutes. Otto slid the bar up to his shirt when the upper body pat-down was completed, leaving only the lower third of the bar below his belt line. Kincaid hurried through the hated duty, giving Otto clearance almost immediately.

Otto made haste into the barracks before the majority had been cleared. He put the bar under his mattress. He would deal with a safer place at another time. *I won't hang for killing,* he thought, *but the next man who makes me a night visit will be as close to death as I can get him.*

Chapter 22

OTTO HAD GROWN IMPATIENT with finding an opportunity to talk to Corporal Jan Huber alone. That evening, Huber had been playing in a poker game in the enlisted barracks. As he left to go back to his quarters, Otto approached him.

"Come into the latrine with me."

"I'm going back to my barracks, Becker. I have no reason to use your latrine."

"Just come with me or I'll drag you down there."

Huber saw the fierceness in Otto's eyes that all had seen when Otto called out the "cowards" who had attacked him. Huber wanted no such confrontation. He followed Otto to the end of the barracks and through the outer latrine door. Two prisoners stood at the long metal urinal.

Otto said, "Finish and get out!"

The men finished quickly, glanced at Huber with question, and hurried out.

"Pigs didn't even wash their hands," said the agitated Becker.

Otto pushed the corporal against the door and placed his face inches away from Huber's.

"Do you handle the prisoner's mail, Huber?"

"You know I do, Otto. I pass it out to the men every day."

"Why haven't I gotten a letter, Huber?"

"I don't know, Otto, I just sort it and pass it out."

"Who works with you?"

"An American sergeant named Sanderson. I help him sort out the American mail by name and unit."

"Does he help you with the prisoner mail?"

"No, it comes in a sack from Camp Hearne every other day, and none on the weekend. I sort all of it."

"Has von Hoffmann told you to hold my mail?" Otto studied the corporal's face, seeking truth or deceit in his eyes.

"No, Becker! Why would he do that?"

"You know damn well why he might."

"Does the Obersturmführer write letters to Camp Hearne?"

"He writes lots of letters. I just hand all outgoing prisoner mail to Sergeant Sanderson. The Americans may read it, I don't know. I think it's censored at Hearne."

"Does he write more than two letters a week? The rule is two letters!"

"He writes more than two, Becker. Sanderson never has me return any to him."

"Does he write letters to prisoners at Hearne?"

"That's against the rules, Otto."

"Lots of things von Hoffmann does are against the rules, you dumb shit. Do you see his letters? Are any to Hearne prisoners?"

"I don't look at outgoing prisoner mail, Private Becker."

"You're lying!"

"You know you can't talk to an NCO the way you are talking to me, Becker."

"If I talk this way to von Hoffmann, why would I care how I talk to you? Are you going to sneak in and beat me at night, Huber?"

"I have nothing to do with your dispute with the Obersturmführer, Becker. Nothing!"

"All right, Huber, we'll see. If I find you are interfering with my mail, *in any way*, I will kill you. Do you understand that, *Corporal?*"

"Yes, that is clear."

"As clear as a man can get, Huber."

Chapter 23

THE FORT WORTH AND Denver rail line ran through the south acreage of the McConnell property. The line carried baled cotton, grain, and cattle to and from the huge stockyards in Fort Worth, as well as standard freight of every description. Passenger trains ran less often on the line but were major movers in the civilian travel business, one that had picked up due to the rationing of gasoline that limited private transit. The passenger centerpiece was the sleek, silver bullet express called the Texas Zephyr. The line, like its counterparts across the country, was the almost exclusive choice for troop movements of battalion size to individuals posted to a new duty station or transported to one of the coasts, bound for units overseas. The long-distance movement of prisoners of war was facilitated by train as well.

When the Camp 67 prisoners worked near the railroad line, Otto watched with interest as the trains rolled through the pasture and fields of the McConnell place. Otto had speculated on the prospect of boarding one of the trains and leaving behind the farm and his fellow prisoners, but the trains that hastened past were going at a speed that made boarding a freight car problematic at best. Farmer Mac's pond, which locals called a "tank," was set a hundred yards from the rails, fenced off as were all the tracks to prevent stray cattle from wandering onto the rails and then being scooped up in the infamous engine cowcatcher. More than one good head of beef had met that fate over the years. The railroad had built one concrete tunnel under the tracks, large enough for cattle or a tractor to pass through.

The other access to the south fields was a crossing on the back road into the farm. There, an old and rattling cattle guard prevented hoofed animals from crossing. This road was maintained by the county and was graveled, unlike the shorter front entrance, the private dirt road, a less reliable entrance and exit in bad weather but closer to the main highway.

Otto had walked down to the pond on this day, hoping to watch trains as he ate his lunch. Sergeant Preston was less attentive each day, clearly showing his distaste for the job and with little concern that a prisoner would try to escape. Preston had made clear that he would not tramp through the fields chasing them for any length of time and would shoot them on sight if he did. He had also informed them that the state had set up a bounty for every prisoner captured, dead or alive, a threat Otto believed did not exist. To accentuate his attitude of total control, today he was having lunch with Ed McConnell in the farmhouse, leaving the prisoners to eat in a place of their choice.

As he approached the rail line, Otto was taken aback to see a passenger train stopped on the tracks. As he drew nearer he saw the familiar uniform of the German Army. This was a prisoner of war train! He moved quickly to the fence, then through the barbed wire. As he did so, he saw an American soldier, rifle in hand, standing at the entrance end of each car. He waved at the troops on the train who waved back, likely unaware of the significance of the "P" and "W" on the legs of his trousers. One of the American soldiers yelled at him.

"Where do you think you're going?"

"Excuse me, sir, as you can see, I'm a prisoner like the men on the train. I just wanted to talk to them a moment. I assure you I mean no harm. I just want to get news of my country, I haven't heard from my family for near a year. If I ..." Otto found himself talking rapidly in an emotional blather that apparently convinced the soldier that he was harmless *and* hurting.

"You speak English, huh?"

"Yes, sir."

"All right, no closer to the rail car than you are now. We've only stopped for a few minutes to let another train pass. Do anything funny and I'll put a hole in you. Understand?"

"Yes, I understand."

Otto yelled up in German, "Where are you going, do you know?"

"Mexico!" yelled a fuzzy-chinned youth in a uniform two sizes past his frame.

"I don't think so, Private," said Otto. A German sergeant called out to him from one of the windows.

"What's your name, prisoner?"

"Becker."

"Hallo, Becker. We're going to *New* Mexico, Becker. The child doesn't know the difference, of course."

Otto looked at the young soldier, then down the gathering of soldiers peering out at him. Many were indeed children, J.T.'s age at best. Some of the others were older men, haggard looking and beaten.

The boy wanted to talk. "Is New Mexico a better country than Mexico?"

"It's not a country, *sohn*. It's a state in the United States."

"Is that good?"

"Well, I guess you could say yes. It's closer to Mexico than where you are now. Mexico is closer to Central America and Central America is closer to South America, so I guess you could say that's better."

"Jump on board," said the teenager. "You can go with us."

Otto smiled. To escape, as the boy indicated, he would have to disguise himself as a *German soldier.*

"*Danke,*" Otto replied.

"Now sit down, Private," said the German sergeant. "I want to talk to this man."

"My God, Sergeant. I've never seen such a bunch, children and old men."

"That's what they're giving us now. Scraping the bottom of the barrel. Most of the old men are useless and the young ones are being sent out without training. Some of the young ones will fight but they lack discipline. They try to be heroic and are foolhardy instead. Most of them are Nazi youth types, hardcore Nazis."

Otto nodded. The dead eyes of youth who had seen too much too soon looked out at him. Only the talkative private seemed of his age.

"Where were you captured?"

"A few of us in some shithole valley in Italy. Some of the men on this train were taken in France, Normandy or near."

"I was in the Afrika Korps. We never had troops *this* young. Twenties maybe, but they had training and were good fighters."

"This is not as bad as it gets, Becker. I'm told they're using children, I mean children ten years old or so, in the German cities, antiaircraft batteries, non-infantry duties, but in dangerous positions."

Otto froze. His son was soon to be eight. If the fighting continues, would he be conscripted at some point? The thought sickened him.

"Hitler says we must fight to the end," the sergeant spat out. "If we're using children, I'd say that is the end."

"I have a child not much younger," said Otto. "Let me ask you before you have to pull out. Are any of the men in the car from Dresden?"

The sergeant's voice boomed out. "Anyone here from Dresden?" There was no answer.

Otto left without another word and ran down the line of passenger cars yelling, "I'm looking for a soldier from Dresden. Anyone from Dresden? Anyone heard what's going on there?"

A voice yelled out as a train sped past on the opposite tracks.

"I'm not from Dresden but I've heard they're bombing the hell out of it."

"Anything else?"

"No, sorry."

Otto continued to move down the cars. He had worked himself into a desperate frenzy. "Dresden? Dresden?"

At that point, an American guard stopped him. "Back across the fence, Fritz. You've had your visit."

Otto's passion could not be contained. "You men in there," he shouted, "what is happening in Dresden? Someone *must* know!"

The train began a lurching start, then began to roll away. Otto could only stand and watch. Some of the prisoners waved a goodbye but Otto found himself unable to respond in kind.

Chapter 24

OTTO ARRIVED BACK AT the work site in a foul mood. Thoughts of children fighting and a bombed Dresden had put him on edge.

"Where you been, Becker?" snapped Sergeant Preston.

"At the pond, brushing my teeth."

"They call that a tank, not a pond, wise guy."

"No, it's not a tank. I know tanks. You didn't direct us where to eat so I had my meal there. And you had yours inside with china and silverware, right?"

"Doesn't matter where I had it, Becker. You're the prisoner, I'm the guy walking around locked and loaded. I eat where I want to, you eat where I tell you."

"And did you get to drink the same water as the farmer, Sergeant Preston?"

"What are you talking about?"

"You Americans, that's what I'm talking about. You have water here only you can drink, water only prisoners can drink. Kumpel could have separate water as well, if he wished. And in the village you have a water fountain for the whites and another for the black person."

"In Warner?"

"Yes, the village you call Warner."

"How the hell did we get on to the drinking water in town? I'm a soldier, Becker. I don't have anything to do with Warner."

"But why do your people refuse to drink with the colored people?"

"That's just the way it is in the South. I'm from Michigan, we don't do it there. Where do you get off on lecturing me about blacks, colored people, niggers, and whatever else they call them? People here do it their way, that's all. None of my business. I don't make the rules. Did you vote on concentration camps, Becker? Well, I didn't get a vote on segregation, either."

"A weak excuse, Preston. Isn't this the land of the free?"

"If I agreed with you it's wrong, I couldn't do anything about. It's getting better. We have colored units in the Army and Army Air Force too."

"But separate, right, Sergeant?"

"Listen, Becker, are you trying to start a fight? Sounds like you been waiting to have your little say on this and you picked today. You think a damned Nazi is going to make me feel guilty when your people are out there rounding up Jews and gypsies and homosexuals and who knows what else? We're not rounding up colored folks and putting them in some concentration camp."

"You already did that, years ago, didn't you?"

"Screw you! You're a bleeding heart trying to make a stand on some mighty shaky ground, Becker. You people blame the Jews for everything. We don't blame the colored man for our problems. He *is* one of our problems but he ain't the blame for them. Answer me this. If you had a bunch of colored people in Germany, do you think they'd be in those camps with the Jews? Damned tootin' they would. About as far from pure Aryan as you can get, don't you think? Don't think you'd find a mulatto chapter of the Hitler's Youth walking round doing that stupid salute of yours, do you?"

"You're hypocrites, Preston."

"Boy, that's calling the kettle black. You're like Zimmerman, yelling at me through the fence the other day about our bombing the cities and killing civilians. Do you dumb fucks understand war? You started this shit and you deserve to have your cities leveled. I know you have a wife and a kid back there and I don't wish any harm on them, but if you think for a minute I care about bombing you Nazis into oblivion, you got another think coming. I think you're a pretty good guy, as prisoners go, Otto, but don't try to switch things around like we're the reasons you Krauts are here in this prison. Your country could not care less about the colored man in the USA. I never heard of Adolph saying, 'Let's go liberate the black man.' No, he said, 'Let's rule the world. Let's rid the world of anyone who can't pass some genes test,' or some such shit."

"I don't think this argument is getting us anywhere, Preston. I've made my point."

"It was your ballgame, Private."

"Just one thing, Preston. I am not a Nazi."

"Yeah, and I was never a slave owner, Becker, so save your sermon for some cracker who cares. And by the way, Becker, in a couple of months the black man will be out here pulling cotton right alongside you. Then why don't you tell him why you're eating like a king and he's having pork and beans from a can and how if he was in Germany he'd be a first-class citizen like you."

Chapter 25

J.T. DREAMED HE WAS wrapped thoroughly in bindings his mother had given him. He was carefully removing them from his body as he stood in front of the mirror, his invisible head, apparently, sitting on the shoulders of the bound teenage body. Soon his entire being would be invisible to the world, and more specifically to Eddie Jackson. He would taunt Eddie first, watch him spin helplessly around as he attempted to find the source of the voice that filled him with fear.

"Why did you play that mean trick on J.T. and Beu, Eddie?"

Eddie gasped. "Who are you? Where are you hiding?"

"I'm right here with you, Eddie Jackson. I've come to get revenge for J.T. Graham and Beu Reynolds."

"No, no, please no!"

"What do you mean, 'No,' J.T.'?" It was not the voice of Eddie Jackson.

"Wake up now. I know you don't have to go to work but I'm leaving you a list of things I want you to do for me and Grandma before I get home tonight." J.T. moaned.

"I wish you'd a just let me finish my dream first, Mama."

"You daydream all day, J.T. You need to rest that brain of yours at night. God will use you as he sees fit, so you need to be content with that and don't waste your time off in some comic book world."

"You dream about Thad gettin' home okay, don't you, Mama?"

"That's praying and wishing, J.T. There's a difference. Now get washed up and have your breakfast. I'm leaving, hear?"

"Yes, Mama."

It was near noon before J.T. finished Mama's list. Beu had come over to pick him up.

"Come on, J.T. You're as slow as Moses. I got those crawdads we caught in the fridge at home. We're gonna fry them up and have a picnic."

"What about Miss Reynolds?"

"She's in Dallas and my dad's working. It's just you and me, Blondie."

Beu had a dozen crawdad tails in a covered bowl he removed from the electric refrigerator. J.T. marveled at the large white fixture. His family had a wooden icebox. Once a week the iceman would arrive in his truck, sink his metal tongs into a 25-pound block of ice, and hoist it onto his back, which was covered with a protective leather shield that resembled a leather apron hung from his broad shoulders. He carried the ice into the house, placed it in the cooler, emptied the pay envelope on top of the icebox, and proceeded to his next stop. Food in the box stayed cool, never cold, and Mama had to be sure its contents were eaten in a timely manner. Before rationing, when there was butter it stayed soft and easy to spread. The margarine, with ingredients unknown to most who used it, took to the icebox temperature in a different way.

J.T.'s day off had been prompted by the prisoners' absence due to base inspections and medical exams. Ed McConnell had wished him a good work holiday by reminding him that there was no such thing as a paid holiday, but, by all means, have fun. J.T. took it in stride. Just another thing. The early teens were a completely puzzling, frustrating time, the rules vague, the expectations mixed, the outlook for feeling a part of things, adult or child, unsure as the stock market in the year of their birth. *What is it I'm to be doing at fifteen?*

"You're almost a man now."

"No, you can't do that. You're just a kid."

"Well, I'd expected more from a young man your age."

"Go out and have fun. There's plenty of time to grow up later. Enjoy these years while you can."

"'Bout time you grew up, boy!"

It seemed like playing marbles and tops had gone first. The sack of marbles J.T. had won sat in the box behind the couch, no more challenges to relieve him of the beautiful cat's eyes and agates had come forth. His killer top that had split more than one opponent into pieces lay with the marbles. Yo-Yos were passé, the hours of perfecting "Rock the Cradle" and "Walk on Home" seemed to have been spent centuries ago. Beu had said comic books were next, so watch out. The great thing about hanging out with Beu was you never had to worry about things like that. You just acted silly or talked about what you were going to do someday or what you did yesterday. Today they were going to eat crawdad tails fried in bacon grease.

"They look good, Beu."

"How 'bout that smell? And this is just the main course. I got Velveeta cheese and light bread to go with it, and raw turnips if you like to eat 'em that way."

"Beu, I wish you cooked for the school cafeteria."

"Yeah, probably a lot more people would eat there if I did."

The boys took their plates out to the back porch. Beu poured them sweet tea with real ice cubes and they moved their chairs close enough to the railing so they could elevate their feet to it. They looked out onto the large yard covered in grass that needed both water and a lawnmower. One large cottonwood tree sat in the corner of the yard providing the only shade. They were content.

Beu looked over at J.T. and grinned. "Okay, I know you have something to tell me, that little dumb grin of yours. You'd make a pretty cretin poker player, J.T."

"First off, since you ask, I now know why they call Mr. Becker 'Crazy Otto.'"

"Well let's hear it, little graham cracker."

J.T recounted Otto's visit to town, embellishing it with added people and stops Otto might have made, spending a whole day in town.

"That's funny. He really thought they'd give him his regular dinner if he surrendered?"

"Guess so—now, the other thing is—you know I do Ricky Logan's Sunday paper route, don't you?"

"You mean you're still doing that for that lazy shit so he can sleep in on Sunday?"

"It's an afternoon paper every day but Sunday, that's why he pays me to do Sunday morning. Can't get up early to save his hide, he says. Anyway, I have to get up early like every morning, so I can deliver the papers and still get to church by nine o'clock. Easy money."

"You're a sucker."

"That's not why I'm telling you this, Beu. You see, on the route there's this apartment house over on D Street. Some of the pilots who are married live there. I have to deliver in front, then go round back to some other apartments and then back to the front. I just circle the building. Well, last Sunday I was coming round the west side and you know it was hot by seven that day, muggy all night."

"Is this a weather report or a story?"

"So I go by this window, it's wide open, shades are up, and here is this naked woman and man just sleeping there. Beu, Beu, she was so beautiful. I'd never seen a woman naked. I just stood there and stared. The man turned over on his other side so I got out of there quick. Wow, Beu, she was something. I sure hope it's hot next Sunday."

"I've never seen one naked either, but I've seen lots of pictures. I'd say ones with a little bit of clothes on are more exciting."

"You ever kiss a girl, Beu?"

"A mess of 'em, are you kidding? I know you ain't."

"I did so!"

"Who?"

"Susie Andrews."

"Susie Andrews! Everybody in ninth grade has kissed Susie Andrews. She don't count."

"Why?"

"Well, cause she's kissed about a hundred guys, that's why. Think about it, J.T., when you kissed that mouth you kissed about a hundred guys' mouths."

"What do you mean?"

"I mean she was a freshman, like us, and she was going out with lots of ole junior and senior boys. I saw her. Susie Andrews don't count, simple as that."

"Counts for me."

"Listen, J.T., Irene's the only girl we need to think about. Eddie and Poot need to pay for that one."

"The tricks we tried were just cretin. I mean letting the air out of all of Poot's tires. That's third-grade stuff."

"The dog poop almost worked, Beu. You set the sack full of fresh dog poop on Eddie's door, rang the doorbell, and lit the sack on fire. That part went okay."

"Yeah, we didn't think it would be his dad who came out and stomped out the fire."

"Maybe we'll come up with a doozy later, Beu."

"Maybe. Say, J.T., you like football, don't you?"

"You know I do, Beu."

"Well, look at this red dot on the side of my boot."

"What does that have to do with football?"

"Here's exactly how, little Jerome boy. That red dot comes from Sammy Baugh, Slingin' Sammy Baugh."

"Are you nuts, Beu?"

Beu's voice took on a low, intimate tone.

"Here's how it got there, J.T., the red dot from Sammy. My uncle just finished painting Sammy Baugh's barn out on his ranch, bright red, the very red on my boot. Now, he knows how much I like football and here he's just spent a week with the best football player in the world. Now Sammy's a hard-working rancher and he couldn't just stand by and not help paint a little. So he did. Now the last can they opened, Sammy Baugh, Sammy Slinging Baugh, stirred the bucket, got it on his hands, dripped it back into the bucket, I mean it is a Baugh bucket. So they just used a little of the bucket and my uncle asked Mr. Baugh if he could bring the rest back to his nephew, me. So you see that can back by the fence?"

"Yep."

"I stuck my finger, just the tip, into that bucket and put a spot on my boot. I'm gonna wear this spot proudly until these boots are gone."

"You really like Sammy Baugh, don't you?"

"Dedicated my life to his legend." Beu held up the boot closer for J.T. to see the red spot. "You all want one, J.T.? We could be the only folks in this country that had a spot of paint touched by Sammy Baugh."

"Okay, I guess so."

"Come on, then." Beu walked back to the can and lifted its lid and placed it on the grass beside the bucket. "Okay, now what you're gonna do is bend over, just touch the end of one finger and then you put your spot on your shoe, wherever you want it, side, back, your choice."

J.T. bent over the bucket and extended his arm to the bucket that seemed full and unused. As his finger touched the paint Beu shoved his arm in, almost to the elbow, then danced back laughing.

"Sammy Baugh, Sammy Baugh, Sammy Baugh," he shouted, bouncing away from the furious J.T.

"Beu, if I was a cusser like you, I'd call you some pretty bad names right now."

"Sammy Baugh, Sammy Baugh."

J.T. began to chase Beu around the yard. As he got close he slung paint from his arm onto Beu's backside then closed the gap between them enough to club Beu in the back of the head with his dripping red arm. Beu fell to the ground and J.T. was on him, smearing paint on his face and arms. They both were laughing now. They wrestled a minute more, then Beu conceded.

"Okay, okay, I give up," he gasped, then laughing again, rolled to his back. J.T. lay beside him, beginning to choke from his own laughter.

"You shoulda seen your face when I put your arm in."

J.T. answered with his half giggle, part laugh, which had always endeared him to his family and Beu.

The boys lay beneath the tree, the sun finding access through slivers created by the wind, opening and closing with the breeze.

Beu reached over to J.T.'s arm and scratched K-U-M-P-E-L in the paint. J.T. smiled, then closed his eyes and lay still for several minutes. Finally Beu broke the silence.

"I wish we could do that to Eddie and Poot."

"We just did ... in my dream."

Chapter 26

PHILLIP PAYNE JOINED THE U.S. Air Corps in 1928. Already a seasoned pilot of light aircraft, he had been inspired by the Billy Mitchell story. However, the opportunity to fly larger and more varied aircraft was his primary motivation. Commissioned a lieutenant, Payne did just that, learning to handle everything from biplanes to bombers. The growth of the Air Force, a support force under the command of the Army, was slow and promotions almost nonexistent until the middle '30s when the country became aware of the buildup of military machines in Asia and Europe. Shortly after, the pace turned to frantic as war seemed a possibility to some, a sure thing to many. In the year 1940 it appeared the United States would soon be at war. Newly promoted Captain Payne was billeted for training with the 48th Bombardier Group in Georgia, then to England in 1941. The Air Units sent to England were trained in the early months by the RAF, which had been flying missions a full year before the Americans arrived.

The early combat history of the 8th Air Force is one of a tremendous loss of planes and personnel. Their percentage of casualties was higher than infantry on the front line. Payne's luck ran out in late 1942 when he was shot down over France, suffering major leg and back injuries. Unable to walk, he hid for three days before a French Underground rescue and subsequent return to England. While recovering in an Army hospital in New York he was awarded the Distinguished Flying Cross and promoted to Lieutenant Colonel. Upon his release, the damaged flying ace was able to convince his superiors he would still be able to teach and command. And thus the arrival at Warner Air Base, entrusted with his first command, a full colonel designation, and the *career topper* job of "warden" of Camp 67.

Today Colonel Payne was dressed in summer khaki without a jacket. He wore no ribbons, only the bombardier wings attached above his left pocket. At first glance the wings might look like standard flyer's wings but at their center, in a circle, was a bomb pointed down toward the target. He wore a mission crush cap, a symbol of a combat veteran. The grommet had been removed to accommodate the headset and the cap remained pressed into that shape.

Payne was still slim and firm and had learned to walk at a pace that made his limp less obvious. He felt he was still a young man and wanted to remain in the Air Force forever, but he was a pragmatist. If he stayed four more years he would have a retirement, but once the war ended he knew there would be a mass exodus of men who wanted out. Would there be a place for a handicapped colonel who wanted to stay? He was sure there would be opportunities in the civilian world. Commercial air travel would boom, he believed. Whatever was out there, he'd fly a crop duster if that was all there was. Wouldn't swooping down on a crop field be similar to a fighter bomber flying low and releasing on target? He would see.

He loved his job, teaching young men the art of dropping bombs, in an *accurate manner.* The job of babysitting three hundred twenty-five German soldiers, *not one* pilot among them with whom he could discuss air battle strategy, was the bad news. Lately he had convinced himself that had he not met these prisoners face to face, eye to eye, he might have gone an entire war never actually *seeing* the enemy. That "think positive" epiphany was getting him by.

On most Fridays Payne conducted two meetings, a morning one with all officers with commands involved with the base's primary business, learning to "poop the pineapple." In the afternoon he met with four officers whose duties included the shared job of administering an enemy prison camp. Those present were Major John Compton, his second in command; Captain Mark Eads, who was the day-to-day liaison and go-to officer for Camp 67; Major Len Cagle, under whose job description were a potpourri of goodies from supply to the WASP pilots on base; and lastly, Lieutenant Ed Wills, U.S. Army, the head of the guard detachment on loan to Warner

Air Field. The Army Air Force Police answered to Lieutenant Wills as well, their duties: patrolling Warner on "party nights," taking control of wayward airmen detained by the sheriff, and the job of base policing and gate duty.

"Good afternoon, men. For those who weren't at the morning briefing I will now, as an old bombardier is wont to do, drop the bombshell on you with which I led off the morning session. *We are getting beer!*" The officers cheered. "However, it's on a trial basis, see how it sits with the churches in town and how the men, and ladies, handle it when they go into town. Have to give Captain Eads credit for staying with this pursuit, which has him the official Pain in the Ass of the Year with Air Command at Randolph. This is on a trial basis, as I said, and it will *not* be extended to the prisoners at this time. Some rules of game I think we'll have to start with, and we can expand those today if you wish, are that no personnel may leave the base if we can determine they've been drinking and no beer can be taken off base. If they want to continue to pay bootlegger prices in town, we will handle their conduct there as we have previously. Canteen bartenders—doesn't that word sounds strange after five months—*bartenders* will enforce a limit of I think three beers, Len thinks four. We'll see. I'd say we'll face a small problem of prisoners working deals with base personnel for a taste of the barley themselves. I know most of the prisoner bases allow modest amounts of beer to be consumed by POWs, but I think we need to take it slowly with the folks in Warner. Having the sinful stuff on base for the servicemen, first step. We'll discuss step two down the line, if there is a step two. Oh, and yes, *beer* is the only alcoholic drink we'll be serving. No stronger liquor, no mixed drinks. Any discussion, questions?"

"Yes, sir, did I hear a rumor of three beers for enlisted men, six for officers?"

"I think you heard that at the same place you heard I might be transferring you to, Shemya, Cagle."

"Sir?"

"That's a base in Alaska."

"Yes, sir."

"A security report is the initial item on my list. Captain Eads, Lieutenant Wills?" Captain Eads took the lead.

"First, the reports from the total POW counts in the country, 161 escape attempts last month. All escapees have been accounted for. Camp 67 had no attempts and has had only the infamous Crazy Otto Caper, as we call it, since the camp opened. Though it was more a stroll through the park, we had to list that one as an official escape attempt. I might point out that the large majority of escapees are captured in three days or less."

"Stop on Becker a moment, Mark, Ed. Becker troubles me. There's something about Becker's being given that beating and then *nothing*. Don't you find it strange that Becker would take that kind of savaging and not retaliate? He has an outstanding combat record, he apparently tells von Hoffmann where to go, and he just licks his wounds and is silent? Puzzling."

"Perhaps the beating worked, Colonel, and he's fallen in line with the von Hoffmann program."

"Maybe, but that's a *big* maybe for me. Watch that development closely."

"I will, sir. Getting back to escapes and security in general, I think we can expect some movement in the escape category sooner than later."

"Why do you say that, Mark?"

"Aside from the Geneva Convention item, that says it is the *duty* of captured soldiers to escape, there are other indications."

"I would think ninety-five percent of the prisoners are not aware of the Geneva Accords except what the Red Cross has told them, and there would be no reason for them to be talking escape with the POWs."

"I believe you're right, Colonel. The factor that concerns me are the incidents of violence in the barracks in view of our small number of prisoners."

"Von Hoffmann!" spat Wills.

"Yes, he and the Nazis in the mix."

"Why don't we just send him to Alva, Colonel. That's where they keep most of the identified SS, isn't it?" said Wills.

"It's a six of one, half dozen of the other, Ed. He creates a lot of tension in the barracks, but the discipline is tight and he's the cause of that as well. I know the guards hate him as much as the prisoners but the prisoners are well behaved, if a little bruised now and then. Let's think about it for a minute. What real harm can he do? You don't like him and neither does anyone else, including his troops I would think, but this isn't some sort of popularity contest. He's a mouthy little weasel who is not about to lead any uprising, but with him on board we have a relatively disciplined and obedient group of prisoners."

"They were before he came. I think we need to ship him out of here. Someone's going to get killed at some point. Your question about Becker could be prophetic."

"I'll take that under advisement."

"Continuing, no sabotage reported. Prisoners working successfully at the motor pool, the bombing range, hanger duties. My worry is the feeling of restlessness among the prisoners. Routine's starting to wear, this is over a year of internment for some of these men. You might see some attempt an escape just for the hell of it."

"You see them trying, huh? It's a pretty good little walk to *anywhere*, as I see it."

"They don't have to walk if they steal a vehicle. And here's a new item. Sergeant Preston, who's a chaser on the McConnell farm, says the prisoners stop working and look with a *lot* of interest every time they're working near the railroad tracks there."

"Hop a freight? Interesting. And what are the chances of that?"

"Preston says there's no way unless the train slows down for something. Goes through too fast to jump on board."

"So someone or something would have to slow the train down?"

"Yes, sir."

"I would think we'd have to take our chances in this one. The railroad is not going to do something unsafe just because we're afraid someone will hop a train."

"I would think they still have a number of railroad security guys left over from the hobo days of the '30s. A POW would likely get rousted at the first stop."

"I'd say those tough boys are in the service right now."

"I can't see Uncle Sam giving a deferment to able-bodied men to chase hobos."

"You have a point, Colonel."

"Anything else on security?"

"Yes, sir," said Lieutenant Wills. "I'm still understaffed on guards. The thing that stretches us is the one guard to ten or more POWs on the farms. We could send more prisoners but the farms don't need many more than that except at harvest time. If I don't get more men, I may have to combine work groups and just service four or five farms at a time on a rotating basis."

"Very well, we'll see how that plays out. Anything else?"

"That's all on security, sir."

"Okay then, Major Cagle."

"A couple of small things, Colonel. The Red Cross is urging us to have more educational opportunities for the prisoners. Right now we have Becker teaching English classes and Sergeant Schneider, wood carving."

"What do you suggest?"

"The Red Cross says correspondence courses with universities are available."

"Language problem?"

"They must have them in German to be able to offer."

"Okay, continue to work with the Red Cross. I think they're thinking in terms of large camps with several thousand prisoners, but it's fine with me."

"One prisoner who works on a farm has befriended a dog. Wants to bring him into the compound as a pet."

"Lord, if it isn't one thing it's another. Should we try that?"

"We could on a trial basis, Colonel."

"Okay."

"As you know, a couple of the churches in town have offered to let the prisoners come into town on Sundays for services."

"I've already discussed that with the mayor. We think the pastors are okay with it, but many of the parishioners would be uncomfortable with their presence. That one's still a no."

"Moving on, then. There's the issue of the barracks heat. No insulation and tar paper walls make it pretty hot in there."

"Already talked to the Red Cross about this. Red Cross even requested fans. Put both those in the "In Your Dreams" folder. They think it's hot, wait till they spend a West Texas winter in there. Next?"

"Well, they want German movies. I told Captain Müeller I had no idea where to get them and he should be happy that his troops are learning English watching the ones we show them. I've been choosing movies that give them an idea about this country, how democracy works, that sort of thing. Their favorites are the cowboy movies, by the way."

"Did von Hoffmann request some horror stuff, *Wolfman, Frankenstein,* some vampire stuff with lots of blood?" quipped Wills.

"Yes, and in color, he said. Black-and-white blood just doesn't do it for him."

"Okay, wisenheimers, move on. The war will be over before we finish."

"Again, petitioned by Captain Müeller for his men to have their own canteen. They point out, as always, that Camp Hearne, Camp McLean, etc., etc., have their own."

"Yes, and they have over three thousand prisoners in those camps, too. We have three hundred fifty. What's the matter, service not good enough for their lordships?"

"Might save our guys from having to deal with them, Colonel. They say they can order from the base lists. They have the idea they could see a profit and with it buy games, records, books, and so forth, for the barracks."

"Where would we put a canteen, Mark? Build another building, a little kiosk selling lederhosen and copies of *Mein Kampt?* Anyway, doesn't the Red Cross supply all those items?"

"Some of them, yes. I'll look into a space for a canteen, Colonel, and we can take it up again another time."

"Thank you."

"Related items: request for Ping-Pong tables or a pool table. Believe it or not, the Red Cross would come up with either or both if we cleared it."

"Mark, I've already got the mayor on my back about the Fritz Ritz thing."

"Just saying, sir, all goes back to the occupied mind versus the idle one. Busy prisoners create fewer problems, in my view."

"You've become quite an advocate for them, haven't you?"

"I'll tell you, sir, we may have these guys here another couple of years, even if things go well in the European Theater. It's just like we've said before about the escape outlook. They're not busy, they're restless; if they're restless there will be trouble, or should I say *more* trouble."

"Well, part of the problem, and I know you've heard this bitch from me too many times before, is the damn NCOs and officers not being made to work. What knucklehead put that in the Geneva Convention rules? So we've got fifty guys sitting around all day with their thumbs up their asses plotting who to beat the hell out of next."

"Hans Schroeder works."

"Wow, sorry, forty-nine guys. What do they do all day? Mark, you've been in that barracks plenty of times, what goes on?"

"Not *completely* sure. They smoke, they read, they write letters, some do crafts. The Red Cross has provided wood and sculpture materials. Heinz is a composer, so he composes."

"I'm sorry, did we buy a grand piano for Lieutenant Heinz?"

"Does it in his head, he tells me. Hums, then writes it down. A small piano might be a good addition, actually. We've let him use the one in the chapel a couple of times. He's talented, Colonel."

"That little heinie has a pretty impressive row of medals on that uniform when he dresses for one of their occasions. I think maybe he has other talents besides music."

"Seems like a very calm, serene man, don't you think, Ed?"

"Yeah, well those are the ones you have to watch. Slip a bayonet between your ribs while he hums Beethoven's Fifth."

"Before we leave the NCO and officers, sir, they have petitioned again for the same pay as those prisoners who work."

"That's one thing the Geneva Convention, or whoever made the rule, got right. Equal pay to the guy who's out in a cotton field all day sweatin' like a fat fry cook. If I could, I'd give them *nothing* unless they worked."

"Do I take that as a 'No,' Colonel?"

"The German officers have said they would supervise enlisted men while they work, remember that, Mark?"

"I remember, but what's to be gained? We have guards with the field hands and the on-base workers are supervised by Air Force personnel. I think they just can't get over the fact that they don't control every aspect of their troops' lives now. I think the enlisted men like the freedom, the time spent away from von Hoffmann and his Nazi boys."

"Boy, we are on a segue run today—and that brings me to ... Ta-Da! ... a *related* item. The men want more of a variety of assignments, some sort of rotation so they get to do different jobs."

"And how long have they been on these jobs—twenty-six years?" snarled the colonel.

"They say most of the jobs are boring, Colonel. They feel stuck in the one routine, they don't like Sergeant So-and-So, they have skills that could be used better in this job, that job, whole list of reasons about as valid as those I've just mentioned."

"I will refrain from saying *tough shit* this time and address this item like I really cared," said Payne. "First off, we would be in a constant cycle of retraining someone for a job someone else just mastered and that would mean more work and time for our men. Tougher to keep track of who's where, who's here, who's missing. Mini logistics nightmare even if it is just three hundred men or so. I'll give you one bone you can throw them. Tell them Colonel Payne will *consider* a rotation system of some sort as long as every enlisted man rotates into farm labor at some point. Faced with folding towels in the laundry or swinging a pick and manning a hoe or shovel, I do believe that request will disappear faster than a Herman Goering steak dinner."

"Before we finish, Colonel," asked Captain Eads, "shall I have Goldberg make the announcement on some of the decisions we've made here today? You know they're shipping him out in two weeks."

"I know. So, let him stick in the knife and twist it one more time, you think?"

"It *is* the most entertaining event on base, Colonel."

"Very well."

Lieutenant Adam Goldberg had been an opportunity too perfect for Colonel Payne to pass up. The lieutenant was the only Jewish officer on the base and spoke fluent German. Payne had used Goldberg to convey all his messages to the prisoners ordered to gather in the compound. Goldberg had been a New York stage actor before joining the Air Force. In his best stage voice, Goldberg would boom into one of the tower microphones: *"Achtung, Häftlinge von Lager 67. Ich bin Leutnant Goldberg!* Attention prisoners of Camp 67 … I (dramatic pause) *AM* LIEUTENANT GOLDBERG! The colonel has asked me to convey the following messages …" To the seething prisoners below, he had become the hated messenger of their captors.

"I'll just toss this in, *as always,* Colonel. They're still bugging us about interrogation of the prisoners."

"They think we have time and the expertise to do that? I've expressed a negative to Command on that a half dozen times. Why doesn't the FBI come out and question these men, who, by the way, have been grilled at every stop before they arrive here? They have a special agent in town because we have a base *and* a prison. We've seen him, what, twice maybe? Let him do it. Just ignore them, Mark, unless we get some sort of specific direct order."

"Begging your pardon, sir, but questioning *might* lead us to be able to separate the Nazis from those who aren't. That would be a good thing."

"Again, I just don't see us having the time or people trained in interrogation."

"Yes, sir."

"Go ahead, Ed, tell the colonel the Number One request on the hit parade."

"Sorry, I'm up for promotion in six months. You tell him."

"Okay, little kiss-up. So Colonel, the prisoner 'command' …"

"Which means von Hoffmann," Ed added.

"The 'command' has volunteered their troops to stand guard duty to give our boys a break!"

The colonel's face fought against the smile that unwillingly turned to laughter. The other officers joined in. As often does, the need to keep decorum in the presence of authority only fed the laughter. The colonel brought himself under control.

"Gentlemen, I think we'll quit on that one. You are dismissed."

Chapter 27

THE SUNDAY SUN WAS like an added punishment, one in which the breeze seemed to be taken away in increments like the tightening of thumb screws meant to solicit a confession. Tension at the camp was palatable. Shared anger, fear, and uncertainty had fermented into a mass with nowhere to go, lacking only a man or an incident to act as its detonator. August gave no physical relief, either by day or night, while the frequent violent and verbal clashes of the two camps, Nazi and those who were not, ramped up the psychic hardship. The beatings occurred weekly now. Derisive notes of warning were left on bunks and intimidation waited around every camp corner.

Amid the weeds a flower or two had emerged. A piano had appeared in the mess hall, wanded there by someone's magical wave. Actually, the magician was Captain Mark Eads, who had engineered its purchase from an estate sale in Warner and paid for it with a combination of funds from the base canteen, the churches of Warner, and the Red Cross. For a week now, Heinz had sat on its ornate bench playing Bach, Beethoven, Mozart, and his own compositions for the mess hall diners. The dinner hour had become a period of peace and nostalgia for the homeland. For that brief period each day the savage breast in each of the prisoners was soothed.

Otto Becker had made a contribution as well. On several occasions he had brought back watermelons to be served to the prisoners. Ed McConnell had planted them at the ends of dozens of rows of cotton. They were placed there for the pickers who would soon be in his fields. It was said that nothing was better than to lay down a cotton sack, break open a watermelon, and gouge out its meat with your hands, liquid refreshment that satisfied the thirst for water which could be hundreds of yards away. Due to the unusually hot weather many of the melons had ripened early. Given an abundance that could not be consumed by his workers, Farmer Mac had given Becker permission to take a few back to Camp 67. Hans had distributed the slices on a first-come basis.

The effort continued to distill an alcoholic drink that could be ingested and remain in the body long enough to effect the desired euphoria. Apples, corn, and potatoes had been tried but Hans and his advisors seemed to lack the moonshiner's knack for brewing. "Three hundred Germans," Otto had chided Hans, "and not *one* knows how to make beer!" One brave tester of the concoctions had been hospitalized and two others had abruptly emptied the contents of Hans's last two meals. The hospitalized drinker had been joined by a young prisoner who had obtained a bottle of shaving lotion from the canteen. Noting its alcohol content, he had chugged the entire bottle. Camp brewmeisters had gone back to the drawing board.

Otto waited for the hammer to come down. Someone in the general area of his bunk was going to get badly injured, perhaps killed, and he preferred it not be him. Von Hoffmann and those who propped him up had not forgotten. Menacing looks and mumbled words of threat happened just enough to keep him alert and ready. One note had been left on his bed which said, *"We have not forgotten your insolence and traitorous words, CRAZY OTTO."* Other prisoners avoided him, either in fear of him or fear of being mistaken as an associate. Huber watched him with a wary eye and when, once again, he had passed out the mail containing no letter for Otto, he would pleadingly look at him and shrug his shoulders.

Otto thought it all to be so childish, had the participants not been so deadly. Rather than gathering together to make the conditions in the camp better to live out the months or years they would be here in as much harmony and comfort as they could create, they sought the opposite: fear, tension, physical danger. Instead of friendship in a common cause there were little notes, pouty glances, and insults. What next, writing the names of the children you didn't like in chalk on the concrete walkways? *Hoffy hates Becker Pecker, nana nah na nah nah.* At times Otto craved the release of a good fight. *Tell me what you think of me, I'll do the same, then we'll punch it out of our systems, dust ourselves off, and just agree to disagree for the duration.* The Nazis and von Hoffmann behaved in a manner they had not earned, morally or militarily. They had fought no harder nor loved their country more than those they sought to intimidate and rule. Where was their license?

A few prisoners from the invasion at Normandy and its aftermath had arrived at Camp 67. Other inmates had been transferred out without explanation. Otto surmised it was by request, an asylum of sorts they thought they might find in a larger prison, hopefully free from the poison of their present internment. The Normandy group was not received well. The Afrikan Korps thought all other units were inferior and somehow viewed their surrender as more heroic than any that might follow. Otto believed in the elite status of the AK but could not bring himself to support one surrender being any less demeaning than another. Von Hoffmann took no stand, not wanting to give Becker another opportunity to outwardly oppose him. Becker would soon be dead and the new prisoners would fall in step with all the others. Becker's demise, he believed, would put an end to the Communists' and anti-Nazis' platform of opposition. He saw no equivalent force to replace Becker's blatant disregard for rank and power.

It was Sunday and the grounds of the camp were less populated than usual. The sun worshipers lay on blankets, near nude, already brown as the proverbial, but never seen, berry. Brown berries aside, a football game was in progress between more tan, trim young men, oblivious to the heat. Other than those brave hearts, the prisoners sought the shade of buildings or stayed inside the ovenlike barracks. There was no breeze to offer relief. Otto sat with Wagner in chairs alongside the Unit Two barrack. Otto missed talking with Klaus. He hoped this exile "plan" of Klaus's worked, otherwise wasted, distasteful time spent chasing a friendship with the SS man (Klaus had said the English for SS was Slimy Shit) would be looked back on exactly as that. Hans joined them, a welcome respite from Wagner, whose monosyllabic grunts passing as conversation had begun to drive Becker crazy.

"What is wrong with our friend Klaus, Private Becker?" said Hans.

"He's still angry at me for my outburst, the medal thing. Who knows what else?" Otto could not share Klaus's belief that he could become von Hoffmann's confidant and ultimately his executioner. The only interchange he and Klaus had was an occasional wink and a whispered "Soon, Otto, soon." Klaus and Hans remained close and spoke often, but the threesome's delightful mess hall exchanges, sitting together in shared companionship, awaited a better day.

"There is news of the war," said Hans. "You just have to decide which version is true: that of von Hoffmann, who believes the German Army has driven somewhere just east of Warner, Texas, and the shortwave radio which broadcasts similar information when they can access a German station, or the news brought by the new prisoners who say we are not doing well and the American radio stations which agree with that assessment."

"But there's been a lot of fighting, Hans, since the invasion. We may have turned the tide."

"Yes, that's possible. The Americans even admit the fighting in what they call the Battle of the Bulge was good news for us. Colonel Payne is selling a different outcome, that the battle is all but won for the Allies. He has asked the officers and the NCOs to work. He says those who work will go home first in the plan for repatriation."

"Sent *home*, that would be a classic example of the good news and the bad news, wouldn't it? Since you work, Hans, you would be among the chosen, wouldn't you? Anyone in your barracks offer to work?"

"You must be joking. Von Hoffmann railed against the idea for thirty minutes. He was so furious he again insisted we could overthrow this camp and repatriate ourselves."

"He's still proposing that idiocy?"

"I don't know if he is stupid or it is his plan to keep the troops agitated, alert. False hope is the only result the younger soldiers have gotten from it. But then again, maybe he *believes* it, since he has never been in combat, maybe he is unaware of the firepower that would be needed to take over this base. The fighter planes alone could cut down three hundred Germans in twenty minutes. Is he a stupid man? I don't know."

"And that's just one of the *projects* he is recruiting men for. We humor him. No one really believes we would accomplish that feat any more than an assassination of Lieutenant Goldberg."

"I haven't heard that one."

"Yes, he keeps plotting to kill Goldberg, but I don't think anyone is willing to trade his life for Goldberg's, which they surely would do."

"There is still talk of an escape. Large numbers of prisoners, I think that will happen one day."

"Would you go with them, Hans?"

"What, and quit my day job? Seriously, do you think they would meet with any sort of success?"

"Not for me to say. Would depend on several things, the first of which, large numbers would work against them. They'd need money, food, and some mastery of English. Otherwise they'd be picked up fast, in my opinion."

"I think I'll wait it out. The bread-and-water diet when caught would just about kill me. Remember the American bread, Otto? And the water here contains too much gypsum."

"You're a culinary snob, Sergeant Schroeder."

"Yes, true, true."

"Zimmerman is in bad shape, Hans. He cried most of last evening."

"About the death of his brother?"

"No, now he has a letter from his sweetheart. Seems she is marrying someone else. He was a shellshock case before he came here, then the brother, now the girlfriend. He's a very sad case."

"Too bad. Zimmerman was a good soldier in Tunisia. He was with us the last year in North Africa, fought well. And he is crying over a fráulein, a woman who cared so little?"

"Would you not feel as Zimmerman if your wife left you, Hans?"

"Ha! I'd say auf Wiedersehen and please take your dog with you. It can hump your new husband's leg for a while."

At that moment, a guard from the nearby tower yelled down at them.

"Hey, Becker, been into town lately? I understand the girls can't wait till you come back and have a root beer with them."

"Ah, the aptly named Corporal Hightower, *guten tag*. How's the weather up there in your little wooden box?"

"Better than down there. The sea breeze blows in every day and I watch the birds shit on your barracks. Life is good!"

"That's marvelous. We worry each day about your comfort. Are you still practicing your rifle skills on the rabbits?"

"Damn sure am. Haven't missed a shot yet. Say, why don't you dumb donkeys go out and pick some of them up, add a little sauerkraut and you have a fine heinie meal."

"You feed us beef, pork, and chicken every day and you want us to pick up your dead bunnies. Who's the real dumb donkey here?"

"Only the best chow for a hero. I hear you were some sort of Sergeant York or something. Were you a big war hero, Becker?"

"Yes, it took the armies of three countries to capture me."

"Well, if you ever get the urge to show me how you dodged all them bullets, let me know."

Otto did not reply.

"Did you hear, Crazy Ass Otto? We're getting beer on base and you turds are not. How does that rattle in your empty heinie head?"

Otto did not answer. This was the first he had heard of the notion. He and Hans looked at each other in disbelief.

"Thought that would get your attention." Otto sought a clever answer but he had been checkmated by the grinning guard.

At that moment, Zimmerman burst from the barracks screaming. His eyes were red, wild, animal-like, as had been his scream. He ran toward the compound inner fence, his sounds becoming higher pitched, the raging of a man gone mad. He ripped off his shirt and began to climb the fence.

"Vom Zaun herunter! Get off the fence!" boomed the voices from two of the towers. *Halte order wir schiessen!* Halt or we will shoot! *Halte!* Halt NOW!"

Zimmerman made it to the top of the fence. He rolled over the wound barbed wire, the blood from the razor cuts covering his arms and chest, his pants shredded. He landed hard in *no man's land* between fences and staggered to the outer fence. He began to climb.

"Halte sofort wir schiessen! Last warning! Stop *NOW* or we will shoot. *Halte!"*

"No, Zimmerman, don't do it!" yelled a prisoner.

"Please," said another, "come down!"

Zimmerman continued to climb, his shrieks now moans of pain that were the inner voice of his total misery, not of his slashed body. As he reached the top, two shots rang out. When he didn't fall, two more followed. His body, tangled in the wire, hung there. Otto and a number of the men ran to the inner fence.

"Let us take him down," shouted Otto.

"Stand back! All prisoners stand back, we will take him down."

The men continued to press against the wire. Most had seen many men fall from enemy fire and were hardened to the sight. But Zimmerman! So unnecessary!

"Stand back twenty yards from the fence. *Bleib Zurück!* Stand back *NOW!*" With that, a machine gun burst rippled the dirt in front of them.

"You idiots, haven't you ever heard of a ricochet?" yelled Otto.

"I'll ricochet one off your ass if you don't move back, Becker!" It was Corporal Hightower.

The prisoners moved back and watched in stunned silence as the American soldiers moved into the zone with ladders and began to remove Zimmerman's body. Other guards in helmets with rifles at parade rest advanced into the compound and pushed the prisoners farther back.

"Suicide," said Otto, "he committed suicide."

"Do you really think he was in control of his senses enough to reason that out?" questioned Hans.

"He had to know what would happen. Maybe he didn't want to live and did this for his family. I don't know. There will be some comfort to them that he was killed trying to escape from an American prison camp rather than from slashing his wrists in the latrine. Ah, Zimmerman, you fought too well to die like this."

Von Hoffmann mounted the steps of Barracks One. The quiet gave him full voice. "What you have here is a coward, a toadie to the American oppressors. He was afraid to stay and join the fight to liberate Camp 67!"

"Halte de Mund, du verdammts Schwein! Silence your filthy mouth! Zimmerman was a brave soldier who fought for the Fatherland longer and harder than most of you here, certainly more than you, *little man!"*

There was a collective gasp from the assembled prisoners. Never had Becker been so completely insubordinate, so blatant as to challenge von Hoffmann in this manner.

"Kill that man!" shouted von Hoffmann. "He is a traitor! He is not a German, he is an American lackey!"

A prisoner grabbed Otto by the collar and swung a fist at the side of his head. Otto broke free, swinging wildly at the man's face. A melee followed for brief seconds as the guards, now bolstered in numbers that included the base police, swung rifle butts at the nearest German, regardless of his alliance. The prisoners' pent-up anger and frustration were well documented, but the guards, who for months had listened to taunts and insults, now had an outlet. The prisoners began to be clubbed to the ground. They attempted to retreat and tripped over one another. They seemed to sense that if they fought back against the guards, bullets would follow the blows. They became passive, some raising their arms in yet another surrender.

Otto searched briefly for von Hoffmann, hoping to take the opportunity to beat him into the dust. The Obersturmführer had disappeared.

Chapter 28

O TTO LAY FULLY CLOTHED on his bunk, the iron bar at his right side, his pillow folded to give him a better view of the barracks activity, should any occur. Hans had made him a pot of black coffee and he had consumed an amount that he imagined would keep him awake for a week. They would come, he was sure. No officer, especially one so vain and consumed in his own self-importance as von Hoffmann, could lose face once again. A grand SS lieutenant as well, unthinkable! The prisoners had been somewhat emboldened by Otto's previous challenges, thus the angry exchanges, the notes, the barracks scuffles, the nighttime beatings that followed. Von Hoffmann must realize he is losing control. *My death*, mused Otto, *would invigorate his followers and give pause to his enemies, much as my first thrashing had. The object tonight, if it is to be, would be to kill me. A mere hospital visit would not be enough.*

Otto lay thinking. *This is not Dachau, Obersturmführer. I will not go meekly to my death.* Otto replayed the bizarre afternoon, Hightower's taunting, Zimmerman's tortured exit from this life, and *then* his inability to get to von Hoffmann in time. He doubted any of the American's rifle butts had found the lieutenant's swollen head. Agitate, then hide, you worthless *dreckschwein*, that is your cowardly method. He must talk to Klaus *soon*. He could wait no longer for his friend to eliminate the man. He was already filled with guilt, and a great deal of gratitude, for Klaus's taking up his cause, but it was *he* who had created the problem.

Perhaps von Hoffmann will be a part of the assassination team! If that is the case, he would fight to kill, not to maim. He kept all thoughts focused on battle, attack, survival, and hate for his adversary. No soft thoughts of family, friends, or Kumpel, who had become like a son in these fast-moving months. Let your mind wander and you would be a dead solder, North Africa all over again. But now it was *Germans* who wanted to kill him, so *wrong*, not the war, the cause for which he had agreed to serve, just an upside down, senseless aberration.

Two men walked slowly past his bunk and to the latrine end of the barracks. They had looked in but Otto was sure they could see no more clearly than he. Two shapes slinking by like buzzards circling carrion. Just two! *My, my, Obersturmführer, you do not think much of me, do you? Where is your respect?* Otto answered for the SS. *Last time we sent four men and they had quite an easy time of it. Why overcommit troops for so simple a mission?*

It all seemed anticlimactic, over in three minutes with Otto gasping for breath, dizzy from the furious rush of adrenaline. There *had* been but two, moving quietly to each side of the figure under the white sheet. One carried a pillowcase to cover their victim's face and a heavy club, the killer on the left, a knife. Before they could bend to his body, Otto swung the iron bar against the knee of the attacker who planned to bury a knife in his throat. The man screamed in pain and went to his knees. Otto could see his head now and slammed the bar into the side of it. He leaped from his bunk, stepped over the inert body, and prepared to chase the other assailant but the man did not run, instead came around to meet Otto, club raised. He was a big man but Otto could not make out his face. Otto's first instinct was to smash the club from his hand or engage in some sort of fencing engagement, bar against club, but the need to feel contact led him to charge. Ducking under the club's arc, Otto drove his shoulder into the man's midsection, wrapped his arms around him, lifted and slammed him to the wooden floor. The man struggled for breath just long enough for Otto to take him by the hair and slam the back of his head—one, two, then a vicious third smash into the floor. The man lay still.

"*Fühlist du dich gut, ja?*"

"Remember beating Otto Becker?" Otto picked up the iron rod and began to rain down blows on the joints of the man's arms and legs, then his ribs.

"*Kannst du dich errinnen, wie due den Otto Becker geschalager hast?*" Otto moved back to the first body and began the same methodical breaking of bones.

"*Du bist eine Drecksau! Dreckschwein!*"

Wagner appeared and held Otto's arm, preventing further swings.

"Stop, Otto, you will kill them!"

"*Ja, ja!*"

"*Nein.* Enough." Wagner took the bar from Otto's hand and put his arm around Becker's waist. Even in his fury, Otto could not resist the strong man's grasp. As Wagner pulled him away he kicked the knife attacker in the side before being lifted completely off the floor. Wagner held him and said quietly, "You have won, Private Becker. No need to kill them. I'm going to let you go and then we are going to remove these bodies. Okay?"

Otto did not speak.

"I will not let you do more, so get yourself under control and help me. *Ja?*"

Wagner released Otto, who staggered away, his breath coming in gasps.

Wagner continued softly and patiently.

"I will get the big man and I am going to throw him out the door. You do the same with the one by your bunk. *No more violence,* just do what I say." Wagner bent and picked up the big man as if he were a child, then walked to the door and threw the man almost to the bottom of the steps. Otto followed, struggling as he rolled the unconscious man down the stairs.

"Now the weapons," said Wagner. Otto located the knife while Wagner threw the club and iron rod after the motionless bodies. Otto had composed himself now. He looked at Wagner, who nodded. He then walked to the door and yelled, "Escape! Prisoner escape!" then stepped back into the barracks as the powerful spotlights swung round the compound, coming to rest on von Hoffmann's battered errand boys.

Chapter 29

WHAT PLANS VON HOFFMANN had for escape were not shared with Otto and on the subject Hans remained vague, Klaus silent. Hans only said that von Hoffmann's selection list of approved escapees changed daily. Two recent escape attempts at other POW prisons received national headlines and could not have been encouraging to the plot masterminds.

At a large camp located at Papago Park, Arizona, one barracks contained Nazi U-boat commanders and their crews. Authorities said some of the brightest prisoners ever captured were the men who captained the submarines of the Third Reich. Plans and labor on a tunnel under the fence ("you either cut through, fly over, or dig under") at Papago had gone on for months. Digging took place at night with crews in three shifts. Tools to dig had been issued the prisoners to build a "faustball" or "fistball" court, better known to Americans as volleyball. Some historians still refer to the 178-foot tunnel as the "Faustball Tunnel" because not only were the digging tools obtained to build the court (and tunnel), but the court was the perfect place to dump the dirt each day after the night digging has ceased. Prisoners were seen each day happily raking, removing rocks, and smoothing the soil. The camp authorities were impressed with their enthusiasm.

One night a loud barracks party, followed by a staged disturbance, allowed twenty-five men to exit the camp. They were later said to be the best prepared of escapees authorities had ever pursued. They had forged papers, civilian clothes, money, and food. Realizing that it would be difficult to carry enough food for days of travel, they had toasted large amounts of the loathsome American white bread and crumbled it into a more transportable size. Add water and the fugitive had a sustainable meal. The escapees also had detailed maps, and that was to be their downfall. The two rivers shown on the map were only a few miles from the prison camp. In anticipation of floating down one of them to freedom in Mexico, they had built flatboats they could disassemble, carry, and reassemble for use on the river. The U-boat men had likely pictured the swift waters of the Rhine or Moselle. Instead, when they arrived at the Salt, the first river on their map, they found nothing but mud puddles. The river, due to damming and weather variations, is dry much of the year. They continued another twenty miles to the Gila River, with the same result. The story, which was to have several versions over the years, indicates the submarine commanders sat on the edge of the tiny trickle and cried. At best, they were severely disappointed. Three of the ring leaders remained at large for several days while their comrades, tired, hungry, and disillusioned, surrendered one after another to authorities, ranchers, or whomever would take them in.

The other escape receiving national coverage took place in Tennessee. Four German prisoners of war had escaped and made their way high into the mountains. In their search for food and water they had come upon a small cabin with a few livestock, a well, and a feisty old widow who lived there. As they came into her yard, they were challenged by the old woman carrying an ancient rifle. She told the soldiers to "Git!" They did not, and in fact laughed at the little lady who threatened them. She waved the rifle at them and once again yelled, "Git, you go on and GIT!" Even if the men did not understand the words they could not have mistaken her intent. One moved to go to the well and the old lady shot him. The others fled. When the sheriff had made his way to her cabin he told the old woman that the men she had confronted had been German prisoners. She was distraught, saying if she had known that she wouldn't have shot the man.

"Well, ma'am," said the sheriff, "who in the blazes did you think you were aiming at?"

"I thought they was Yankees."

Chapter 30

SOMETIMES BEU WAS A pain in the behind. Like yesterday, for instance. Beu had picked him up from work and they stopped at the drive-in, where Beu bought J.T. a Coke. So far, so good, but then they'd got to talking about Farmer Mac and how it was a shame he didn't have him some boys to do some of that farm work. Next to a good tractor and a wife who could cook, having about four or five sons who were hard workers seemed to both boys to be essential for a successful farmer.

"Some folks who need kids, like Mr. Mac, can't seem to have any, whereas your folks had six they didn't need."

"What do you mean, Beu, 'didn't *need?*'"

"Well, let's just forget the rest of the Grahams and take you, J.T. You were sure as sugar a mistake, no other explanation for you. Think about it. Your brother is six years older than you, then there are four others older than him."

"Yeah, so …"

"Sooo, you think its 1930 and your folks said, 'Well fiddle-dee-dee, whoop-dee-doo, what'll we do today? I know, let's celebrate this nice ole depression and have us another mouth to feed.'"

J.T. sat silently, turning it over in his mind.

"Truth is, J.T., if parents knew how *not* to have kids, most of us wouldn't be here. Me, for sure."

"And me, Beu?"

"Yeah, you too, Goldilocks."

"My dad says back in the pioneer days some folks killed their babies before they were born, even after, when there was no way they could feed and take care of them. He said it was likely it happened during the Depression, too."

"So me and you are lucky, J.T. The thing is, the Jacksons went ahead and had Eddie and the Meyers didn't know Poot was a mistake until it was too late."

It had been a lowdown discussion that J.T. could have done without. He couldn't argue Beu's point. Here he was, fifteen years old and still sucking at hind tit. Three more years of high school, he vowed, and no one would ever have to spend another penny on him. Mr. Mac said he was a good worker and there would always be folks out there who were looking for a man who wasn't afraid of hard work. Nevertheless, the thought of it all had left him a little blue. At the farm, Otto had asked about his attitude, which contrasted greatly with his. Otto seemed to be in high spirits. J.T. had asked him what he was so happy about and he'd said two of the prisoners in his barracks had a little accident last night. When J.T. had asked him why that made him happy, he just chuckled. Maybe it was like the Crazy Otto story and he'd tell him all about it later.

It had been a hard day. For most of the day they had loaded hay onto a wagon, then unloaded it in the barn, then did it all over again. There were the pigs to feed, slop to be picked up at the base, and the pens to be mucked.

An exhausted J.T. climbed aboard the bus home and collapsed into a seat next to an airman looking at multiple photos of a pretty brunette girl before placing them in an opened envelope, then removing them once again. J.T. wanted to compliment the airman on his girlfriend but had neither the energy nor the motivation to do so nor the ability to voice an apology to him for smelling like pig shit. Earlier the airman had taken a sniff and moved slightly toward the window, and though J.T. sympathized, there was no other place to sit.

When J.T. arrived home, the fatigue and the residue of Beu's shared, depressing thoughts walked in with him. He wanted to just wash up, again, browse the ice box, get a glass of water, and be a useless cretin till bath and bedtime. He was startled, then, when Mama threw her arms around him and danced him across the living room floor.

"I'm so glad you're home, honey!"

"You are?"

"What do you think we got in the mail today?"

"THAD!"

"Yes we did, darlin', at long last a letter from your brother."

"Can I read it?"

"'Course you can. Read it out loud. I've read it, now I want to *hear* it."

Mama handed the letter to J.T., then sat back on the couch and smiled like she was going to hear the reading of a millionaire's will and knew what was in it.

J.T. read.

> *Dear Mama, J.T. and Grandma*
>
> *Sorry I haven't been able to write. I got one letter finished and then it rained so hard that night every part of my body was soaked and the letter was waterlogged and you couldn't make it out. Anyways, I am fine, no wounds or stuff like that you probably worry about. I am in this beautiful country for two weeks on what they call R&R (rest and relaxation). First break in over two years. This is the most beautiful country I have ever seen. My friend Tony says that's not saying much, since all I've ever seen is Texas and California. But it's true, millions of trees, mountains, and rivers. I'm not supposed to tell you what the country is called but our gunny says I can say they're on our side and have some fellers fighting like us.*
>
> *I sure needed this rest. I've seen some pretty bad stuff and done some, too, that I hope God will forgive me for, though I don't know what He really thinks of war (should have paid better attention in Sunday School). Best thing so far about this R&R was taking a bath, to soak the grit off, then a shower to wash it away. You wouldn't have let me in the house the way I smelled, Mama.*
>
> *I know you have rationing, so every time I sit down to one of these great meals I wish I could share it with you. I'm drinking a lot of milk. It's the first time I've had any since we left Camp Pendleton. I'm pretty skinny, so I'll probably leave here ten pounds heavier.*

*J.T., I hope you're doing a good job as man of the house.
I know you're working this summer because you always have
a job. That really helps Mama. I think I should write a letter
just to you about how many pretty girls there are here, and
how friendly they are. By the way, if they fit, you can have
any of my clothes you want. Since Mama saves everything,
I know they're still around. Are they still playing college
football, J.T.? There was talk about not playing because of the
war. Tell Grandma she got me in trouble. My friend Tony is
Italian and at first when I met him I kept saying "Eyetalian"
like Grandma. He had a fit. Tony's from New York and he
thinks I'm a cowboy because everyone from Texas must be
one.*

*I've only been here three days as I write this, so I'll write
again before I leave. I sure miss all of you and Warner and
Texas. Tell the girls I wrote and that I think about them, too.
I love you all.*

Thad

Tears were running down Mama's face. To ask her the childish question of whether he was an accident or not now seemed selfish and unnecessary. If a letter from Thad could bring her so much happiness, it was clear she loved them all. And knowing Mama, *if* she admitted he was a surprise, she'd just say it was a lucky and blessed one.

Chapter 31

THE TWO MEN WILLING to kill Becker to retain control of Camp 67 had been badly injured. Both had been transferred to Camp McLean for the better hospital facilities and to ramp down the tension at the Warner prison. Neither would be returning. There had been a brief inquiry into what had happened, but it was halfhearted at best. In truth, Lieutenant Wills had been happy to rid the camp of two known Nazis who had a close relationship with von Hoffmann.

Colonel Payne had felt the need to show some displeasure in having to deal with yet another physical encounter, puzzling as it was to security that two men of such size and background had been beaten to near death and yet no other prisoners showed evidence of fighting. Fully clothed, the idea that they had been beaten in their bunks seemed unlikely. The barracks were searched; three prisoners were found with weapons and sent to the stockade. Movies were cancelled for a week and the lights out time was moved up to 8:30 for an undetermined period. Otto's English class, which now numbered twenty courageous souls, was cancelled as well.

Payne had dealt with the fight/assault but what to do with Zimmerman's body had been a more difficult decision. It was the first death of a prisoner and there was no precedent. The cemetery in Warner had been adamant that he *not* be buried alongside residents of the county. The bodies of two pilots who had crashed since the opening of the base had been interred in their home towns. Colonel Payne had asked Captain Eads to check with the larger prisons and he had done so. It was decided that Zimmerman would be buried on base property outside the base and prison grounds.

Private Jung, who worked in the infirmary, had seen Zimmerman's body. He told Klaus that all four shots had been kill shots.

"That's something your escape committee should keep in mind, Klaus."

"The distances weren't that great, Otto."

"Nevertheless, those men were chosen for that job for a reason. I think taking out those spotlights before you try to clear the compound would be a priority. If they can hit a running jack rabbit from two hundred meters, they can hit you."

"You give them too much credit, Otto."

"Well, not my ass getting shot at, but too much credit is better than giving them none."

Captain Eads had made the arrangements for the burial. A spot on a rise looking down on the base had been chosen. In a clearing among a thick grove of mesquite trees six prisoners, including Otto and Klaus, had volunteered to dig a grave in soil drained of top covering and heavy with rocks. After the completion of digging, the men returned to the barracks, showered, then put on their German Army uniforms. Otto had only a jacket and a worn, tattered shirt left from the uniform which he was wearing when he arrived in Texas. He attached his Iron Cross around his neck, the medal covering most of his frayed collar.

Captain Eads had asked POW Captain Müeller to select a maximum of twenty men to attend the funeral. Fourteen AK soldiers, including Müeller, stepped forward to participate. Zimmerman had been encased in a wooden coffin hastily built from disparate pieces of lumber and transported by truck to the site while the prisoners marched in step behind it. The POWs unloaded the box and carried it on their shoulders to the grave. Their eyes were forward while a soft cadence guided their steps. Father Murphy gave the formal funeral address, then Otto Becker stepped forward representing the members of Zimmerman's battalion.

Karl Martin Zimmerman did not surrender, nor was he a prisoner such as we. Private Zimmerman died in North Africa when the explosion of bombs and shells rang in his ears and would not stop ringing. His earthly time ended here, but he was a casualty of war many months before that, a brave soldier of the Afrika Korps who served his country and the Korps as both a hero and a tragedy of war.

Bis wir uns wiedersehen, Karl Zimmerman

Gott sei mit dir

To the prisoners' surprise and gratitude, Captain Eads had assembled military police with rifles to fire a twenty-one-gun salute to the fallen soldier. Upon doing so, the riflemen and prisoners returned to the barracks while the grave diggers remained to fill in the grave and place a wooden cross at one end. Captain Müeller had suggested nailing one of Zimmerman's identification tags to the cross but Eads told him it would just be stolen or destroyed. Zimmerman's name and date of birth were painted on the cross while one tag was buried with him and its companion part was to be given to the Red Cross to return to Germany. Eads had assured Müeller that the site of the grave would be carefully entered in base records so that at some point Zimmerman's remains could be sent back to his homeland.

Chapter 32

OTTO'S MANGLING OF THE two Nazis, along with the death and burial of Zimmerman, had ushered in a period of calm that was needed and welcome. It seemed no faction wanted more drama at this point.

The camp came off the punishments administered by Payne, slight as they might have been, and returned to a normal, that is to say dull, day-to-day life. The talk of the AK troops was the rumor being passed that Field Marshall Erwin Rommel may have been among the conspirators in the attempt on Hitler's life. News from the American media had given slight notice to the rumor.

Mail from home continued to arrive, though more sporadic, the land war getting closer to Germany each day, the pounding from RAF and American bombers becoming more intense. No packages from relatives had been seen in some time and that had been a good thing in the eyes of some who felt a guilt in getting any gift that contained foodstuffs while they ate better than the rationed populace of Germany as well as most of the U.S. Otto received no letters. The Red Cross had told him they were still seeking information on his family but had nothing to report at this time.

There had been minor arguments between the AK troops and the late-arriving Normandy group concerning thievery. AK soldiers said the disappearance of personal items had coincided with the arrival of the prisoners captured in France, a group that was mostly teenagers. Utensils from the mess hall also went missing, leaving speculation that this was a part of escape preparation since the items served no use in the barracks.

Otto kept as positive an attitude as he could manage. He knew despair would lead to weakness which might get him killed or induce a sickness of the mind, then the body. He tried not to think of his wife and child, but a Sunday visit by a woman and her daughter, whom he imagined to be Lorenz's age, had left him pressed to the fence until she disappeared into the airmen's visit area with her child. In moments like this, a desperation came over him, a wild need to do *something*, find *some way* to make contact with his family. Joining the group planning to escape, if they would have him, struck him as a pursuit with little chance of success. For the time being he would enjoy Kumpel, an inadequate but often delightful substitute for family.

Otto was in fine spirits on that Monday. He had willed himself so; the barracks defense of his space had been more than a small part of his good humor. J.T. appeared glum that morning, an occasional smile but strangely quiet.

"Why the long face, Kumpel? Charles Atlas didn't make your face muscle bound as well, did he? Is it your love life? Gorgeous sweetheart pressing you to marry?"

"Nah, none of those, Mr. Becker. I don't know, school starts soon, my job here will be over till the cotton comes in, and stuff like that. I'm usually glad for school to start, but not this year. I should be happy, we got a letter from my brother and he's okay. Said he'd seen and done some bad stuff. He was on a kind of vacation from fighting, so that's all real good for us."

"I am glad."

"You are? Ain't the Japanese on your side?"

"That's what they say, but I don't think we could ever coexist if both countries prevailed in their parts of the world. Pure speculation to try to figure out what would happen." Otto realized J.T. wasn't following him. "Anyway, I would never pick the Japanese over the Texas Graham family, bright, muscular, and six strong!"

J.T. smiled.

"That's better. What we need is a song. We have a new one. How's this?

You are my sunshine, my only sunshine, you make me happy ..." At that point, the other prisoners joined in. The group burst out in song frequently during the morning. German songs had replaced the American pop tunes, the prisoners joining in a full-throated rendition of *Die Lorelei* as they walked to the shade of the barn to have their noon meal.

Farmer Mac was waiting. He was frequently in an unpleasant mood but there was real anger in the fierce look he gave the prisoners.

"I'm tired a hearin' you Nazis singing your German songs on my property. What ya got to sing about, you live in a damn prison."

"We were doing your work, farmer. Is there a problem?" Otto asked.

"I don't want to hear your bleatin' all day!"

"Ah, Herr McConnell. Why didn't you tell us we were disturbing your fine American ears? We have lots of songs. How about we sing some American songs for you to feel better and you can sing along as well? Okay? How about this one, Herr McConnell?"

Otto turned to his men and mouthed the name of the song.

"Eins, und zwei, und drei ...

"Old McConnell had a farm

"Eee-yi-eee-yi-oh

"And on this farm he had some pigs ..."

"Shut up, dammit!" yelled McConnell.

"With an oink, oink here and an oink, oink there ..."

Ed McConnell was livid, his face red and puffed with fury.

"Shut your yaps this minute!"

"Old McConnell had a farm ..."

McConnell ran into the house.

"Eee-yi-eee-yi-oh!"

He returned carrying a shotgun which he pointed in the air and fired. The prisoners jumped back and took cover as buckshot tinkled down like tiny metal raindrops on the tin roof of the barn. Only Otto and J.T. did not move.

"Don't shoot anybody, Mr. Mac. It's my fault, I taught them the song."

"Stay back, J.T., this gun is still loaded and I got more shells in my pocket."

"Could you just give me the gun and I'll put it back in the house. I know where you keep it. I promise these fellers won't sing that song again. You can fire me, that would be fair, but don't shoot anybody."

Sergeant Preston came running through the vegetable patch to the barn and stopped short when he saw the gun in the farmer's hands.

"You fire that shot, Ed?"

"I just want them Nazis to shut up! Stop singing!"

"Give me that!" Preston jerked the gun from McConnell's hands like a drill instructor preparing to examine it.

"Christ, Ed, listen to you! You got grown men coming in here and working for eighty cents a day, *hard farm labor,* and you don't want them to SING! You better be damn glad they want to sing instead of wanting to cut your throat. These men ain't Nazis, Ed. Come out to the base sometime, I'll show you real Nazis! These men are here to work for you—they ain't going anywhere, they don't have a home to go to everyday like J.T. Give 'em some slack."

"I gave them watermelons."

"And that was good of you, Ed. But if you are goin' round firing off a weapon, then that *ain't* good. If I ever see this shotgun or any other weapon outside your house while the prisoners are here, that will be the last day you have them. I can guarantee that. Let them sing, or double their pay. Which one of those would work best for you?"

McConnell did not answer.

"I'm calling for the truck, Ed. That's enough for one day."

The farmer went inside the house. Sergeant Preston emptied the remaining shell from the gun and followed him in. The prisoners milled around the pickup area discussing what had just taken place.

Otto went to J.T. and put his hand on his shoulder. J.T. looked up and smiled.

"You were very brave, Kumpel. While the others ran, you faced the danger like a man."

"Ah, I wasn't brave. I didn't think Mr. Mac would shoot me."

"But you didn't know, did you?"

"No."

"One thing you must learn is that an angry man with a loaded gun may do anything, even the unexpected or the perverse. He may do it on purpose or he may do it by accident. Don't take that unnecessary chance with your life. The farmer is an unhappy man and unhappy people are unpredictable. Three days ago at Camp 67 we saw what can happen when there appears to be no worldly end to their unhappiness."

"Well, you were brave too, Mr. Becker, you didn't move an inch."

"That wasn't bravery, Kumpel, that was indifference."

"What's that mean?"

"It means I didn't care."

———————————————————————————

Otto's day of surprises had not ended. When he entered the barracks after the security pat down, Klaus motioned him to the latrine. The facility was half full and conversation space was not to be had. Klaus whispered, "Outside," and Otto followed.

"I can't take long, Otto, they may suspect something anyway, my speaking to you."

"What's wrong?"

"Nothing, I just wanted to tell you goodbye in case I am killed or hung."

"You're talking nonsense."

"No, Otto, I'm not. Friday night I will kill Obersturmführer von Hoffmann.

Chapter 33

I N 1944 THE ART of dropping bombs from aircraft was thirty-three
years old. Most of the men at Warner Air Force Base were not born
when the Italians dropped the first bombs on the Turks in 1911, those
bombs being nothing more than oversized grenades. The planes, methods
of bombing, as well as the ordnance, had advanced rapidly through two
world wars.

The sole purpose of the Warner base was to produce pilots and crews
who could be sent to any war zone and perform, with some success, the
skill of bombing enemy targets. The curriculum changed almost daily.
Information from the Air Force units in combat zones was fed back to the
training bases, where the evolvement of the "book" on bombing became as
fresh as the fuzzy cheeks of the men undergoing training.

Warner's bombing range was suited for low-level, low-altitude bombing
using medium-sized bombers, primarily the B-25 and B-26. There was not
enough acreage at Warner to practice the dropping of heavy payloads. In
fact, most of the ranges in the U.S. could not handle, nor would want to,
saturation drops that were becoming common in Europe, leaving those *live*
runs as the *first* run for many pilots and bombardiers.

Large bombers, even at low levels, were ineffective against smaller,
moving targets like ships so a method called *skip bombing* had been
developed. One simply needs to think of standing by a body of water and
skipping a stone across its surface to imagine the simple idea of doing the
same with a bomb. The delivery of these bombs required precision and a

great deal of courage on the part of the pilot and crew. In some cases, only volunteers were used to man these planes. The term *mast height* bombing was used to describe this procedure and depicted the plane delivering its explosives just above the masts of ships. Control towers of military vessels were the "masts" of the enemy warships and were the aiming point for the pilot. Bomber nose guns and fighter craft, when available, would attempt to clear the target area of antiaircraft guns as the bomber approached at an altitude of two hundred to two hundred fifty feet, the plane geared down to two hundred miles per hour as it swooped down on its target. The drop of the projectiles was made seventy to one hundred fifty yards from the target, where they slithered and bounced silently over the surface of the water. Some who survived these attacks remembered them as not so silent, saying the bomb made enough sound that they remember hearing the hissing of its sharklike approach over the roar of the bomber, now pulled up sharply as it exited the air space above the eminent explosion. Precision was the word. Pull the plane's nose up too quickly and the bomb might go completely over the target; drop it too soon and the explosion might happen yards short. In rough seas, skip bombs had been known to be swept up and back toward the delivering aircraft. Surviving the enemy ground or deck fire was a priority for success. Silencing the guns was aided by the timing of the attack. Skip bombing runs were usually carried out in one of several conditions: first light of dawn, clear moonlit nights, the run made *into* the moon, low-setting sun, low clouds, or poor weather. Fuses were set for four or five seconds and were started by the bomb's impact into the water. Because of the fuse, the hit did not have to be broadside, sometimes the bomb burying itself underneath the target where it blew up, or exploded above, raining death down onto the deck or facility below. Usually two or three bombs were dropped, one after another, increasing the chances of a major hit. Moonlight vision worked well, and if there was none, flares might be dropped for night attacks. Skip bombing across sand or other dirt terrains had not been as successful or widely used. The trajectories were unpredictable, bombs tending to veer off target or be blown up prematurely when they came in contact with a hard surface prior to hitting the objective. Skip bombing, then, became primarily a water technique and was used more in the Pacific war than the European. It proved to be, in all combat areas, an approach that met with great success.

Not all air bases taught bombing skills, even fewer skip bombing. The nearest to Warner was the base at Midland, Texas, and, perhaps the best, located on the Salton Sea in California. The use of Lake Warner for bombing was controversial in the small town. The lake was one of the sources for drinking water and had been a fishing, boating, and picnicking site for locals prior to the war. The war effort trumped all civilian uses of the lake for recreation, though the filtering system still rendered the lake water passable for drinking. It was not delightful mountain spring water to begin with and some local wags said the flour and gun powder might actually improve its taste. The lake was the result of two main creeks that fed into it, as well as overflow of the Red River at peak crests. Warner County averaged twenty-three inches of rain a year, 1944 well on its way to thirty. There were dry years as well, when the still vivid memory of the Dust Bowl, coupled with low crop yields, unnerved some farmers to the extent they prematurely sold off livestock and equipment.

The lake was off limits to civilians, even when not in use by the Air Force. The base command feared some unexploded ordnance may have made its way ashore, thus the safety of lake visitors must be protected. The lake covered eight hundred acres, the maximum depth being fifty feet while much of the shoreline was ten to fifteen feet at the most. A concrete boat launch was the only structure besides a filtration unit which was set fifty yards from the shoreline and was fed by pipes from the lake, then transported by other pipes into the water towers in Warner. The Air Force declared all other areas of the lake suitable for bombing, both of the drop and skip variety.

Ordinarily, the prisoners were asked to work an eight-hour day, forty-hours-a-week schedule. The base command's interpretation of the Geneva rules was that if the "captor" personnel were working longer hours than the prisoners, those POWs engaged in the same activity could be asked to do so as well. Colonel Payne had complained that it was like the POWs had "some damn union." Compensation was expected but an amount was not spelled out. And so it was that Klaus Lang, who was a valued and experienced worker in the area of target site setup and clearing, had been told he would pull night duty in an upcoming skip bombing exercise. Klaus was not surprised, since he had participated in the building of special targets, both those on the lake and those put together on the base and hauled to the site. As Otto had pointed out to him on several occasions, Klaus's job was a dangerous one, one that Swiss and Red Cross observers, as well as the Central Army Air Force Command, would certainly have ruled for the prisoner should one have refused to perform the tasks. Klaus liked the job, the danger being one of his perceived perks. On the main range, Klaus's duties included preparing the site for bombing by arranging targets and cleaning up debris left from the previous day. When all bombs had been dropped, Klaus went out onto the range with flags of different colors attached to metal sticks which he placed in the ground at impact areas where a shell casing, which had been loaded with sand or flour, lay on its side or buried in the ground. Unexploded bombs, even those loaded with only a nose charge, were marked with a red flag. Bomb removal squads would deal with their removal or detonation. After *live* bomb runs, the danger to Klaus, as he made his way through the range, increased a hundred fold.

There *was* an aspect of his part in the training of the bomb crews that bothered Klaus more than the danger of the job. He was assisting in preparing men to bomb his country and its army. But what were the men to do who were *required* to work? Refuse and you lived on bread and water for the Geneva maximum. Refuse again and it would be back to the stockade. In truth, all jobs performed by the POWs helped the Allied war effort. Otto helped produce food for home consumption and troop rations, cotton to clothe them; the hospital orderlies tended to the enemy. It was the nature of being a prisoner, easy to criticize by NCOs and officers but a rock and a hard place for the others. Tonight, at least, he hoped to use his bombing range work as a problem solver. Guilt would be exchanged for the good of Camp 67 and his fellow prisoners.

It was a special night for the pilots and bombardiers, much like a final exam. Live bombs would be used, no flour, sand, or concrete; fuses would be set with precision; the low level "mast head" runs would have to focus on the targets, not the flashing lights simulating ground or deck fire. Explosions would rock the lake like a July 4th gone crazy. Pilots, used to dropping their harmless bombs to develop precision, would see *real* results, of a sort, not an oil tanker or an enemy destroyer, but solid structures that would go boom in the night giving them results from their runs that could be seen and measured. It would be a special Friday night for *many* people.

Klaus was sick of toadying to a man he detested, but there was no other way to get close. Von Hoffmann had been amused that Klaus wanted to join his camp, his pleasure came from having men resist, then bend to his will, enjoying even more the punishment or elimination of those who did not bend. Klaus had realized what was good for him, the Obersturmführer believed. Becker, who still resisted, would be eliminated. Klaus's first conversation with von Hoffmann, and those that followed, had as their common denominator the condemnation of Otto Becker. The very mention of the rogue private could drive the SS man into a red-faced stomp.

"Your friend ..."

"Former friend, sir."

"Private Becker will be dealt with. He was fortunate to survive the last visit. You are correct in distancing yourself from him."

"Yes, sir."

"What is your work with the Americans, Lang?"

"I work on the bombing ranges, sir. I spot unexploded bombs, help clear the area, build and fix targets."

"Ahh, Private Lang, perhaps you have information I could forward to our army and the Luftwaffe."

"I would be happy to share anything I know, sir, but it would be best for you to observe the bombing tactics and planes yourself."

"How would I do that?"

"From time to time we use extra prisoners to work. Those are usually for the live bombing drills."

"I do not work, Lang!"

"I know, sir, but if you could make an exception for one day or one night, I think you could gather valuable information. The High Command would be most grateful to you, I'm sure. You wouldn't actually have to *work*. Hortz Frank and I would handle it, you could observe."

"Keep me informed, Lang. Your proposal interests me."

Klaus knew from experience that extra prisoners or base personnel were needed for night bombing on the lake. When Wing Commander Nichols made his request, Klaus was quick to submit Private Bernhardt Wagner and Obersturmführer Werner von Hoffmann. Major Nichols had questioned a lieutenant volunteering for work. Klaus gave an answer of partial truth, that Colonel Payne had been urging the German officers and NCOs to join the work force and Lieutenant von Hoffmann had responded. Major Nichols, like most of the base personnel, had no contact with the POW camp other than his use of the prisoners for work. Von Hoffmann's reputation had not preceded him.

Eight targets had been prepared for individual attack by the B-25s. A recently created tradition of the live skip bombing exercises was that the ground crew was allowed to name each target. One target, donated by the Warner School district, was an old school bus, beyond repair, dragged to the edge of the lake and christened "The Little Yellow Slit-Eyed School Bus," another, two "ships" constructed of empty oil drums stacked in a manner to resemble a floating vessel. In their short life span, they would be known as "Gene Krupa" and "Buddy Rich." Two docks had been built extending twenty feet out into the lake and backed by a concrete block five by ten feet. They were "Dock Holliday" and "Dock Pepper." Two more concrete duplicates of the dock pieces, minus the dock, were placed separately in the shallows and called simply "Tokyo" and "Berlin." The last target had been conceived to use up some of the excess timber that had been shipped from Denver and piled lakeside. Previously, logs had been tied together and floated on the lake. The flat target had proved to be less than ideal, leading Klaus to conceive and help build a vertical target that became known as the "Bavarian Forest."

A raft was built of eight logs, seven feet in length, arranged in two rows, intertwined and attached to each other at that point. This had been the design for the original floating target but had been difficult to see and hit. Klaus's design added eight logs, or four pairs, *standing* and leaning against each other at a slight angle, allowing them to be attached at the top and giving some balance to the structure. They were separated six inches apart and secured to the raft at their bottoms. Two-by-fours running along the tops and cables on each end prevented their falling to the side and off the raft. Other wooden pieces were attached at points of need, resulting in a Rube Goldberg contraption that was bizarre but sturdy.

Five of the eight targets were spaced around the shallows of the lake; the two "ships" and the "forest" were to float separately, arranged so that each would take an individual bomb run. The bombing runs would require approaches from several different directions and be in need of an alert, competent crew in the control tower. Though only one craft would be bombing at a time, the planes *were* being flown by pilots still in training and controlling the air traffic could become a bit hairy. For that reason only two planes would be in the air at one time, the others awaiting takeoff at the base. The lake control tower was a simple one, a rickety version of the towers on base and at the main bomb site. It was on as high a ground as could be found, twenty feet in height, and distanced from the lake a hundred yards. It was located on the filtration plant end of the lake for personnel safety, and it was a *no fly* zone for the bombers. Major Nichols's recurring nightmare was not so much a hit on the tower as his fear that a rookie pilot might bomb the pipeline or the filtration plant. There would be hell to pay if that happened. Major Nichols would direct the runs and observe the success or failure of the attack. A sergeant kept contact with the planes prior to their takeoff at the base and while they were in the air waiting to be turned over to Major Nichols's direction. Another enlisted man, in communication with the Air Force ground crews at the lake, was the voice of the PA system and keeper of the siren that signaled "Clear the site" or "All clear on the site, you may proceed."

Two small motorized boats were being used to transport the prisoner teams who would pull the floating targets into place, anchor them, and check the shoreline targets. Hortz would tow both Krupa and Rich onto the lake and check the bunkers, Tokyo and Berlin. Final check of the land-based targets consisted of testing the lights that would flash into the bomber pilots' eyes. The green battery-fed lights on the floating targets were already in place as they were towed out. Hortz Frank, who worked on the bomb sites each day with Klaus, "captained" one boat, joined by two prisoners he had recruited. Captain Klaus's motorboat carried him, Wagner, and Werner von Hoffmann.

"All right," yelled Klaus over the noise of planes already in the area. "We'll go check the two docks and the bus, then tow the timber target out." Klaus was careful not to give its anointed title, seeking not to excite the Obersturmführer before he needed to be excited.

"There are so many targets on a small lake. It seems very disorganized if there is to be one plane for each target," sniffed von Hoffmann.

"Not ideal, of course, sir. But in this part of the country there are no large bodies of water. Perhaps what you'll be able to communicate back to your superiors is the disorganization of the Americans as well as their tactics. Now, we need to complete our tasks quickly so they can begin."

"What am I learning here, Lang, how to take a ride in a motorboat?"

"Oh, I think you will find it instructive before we are done, sir."

Klaus made a quick run to the bus and docks, needing every minute to put the Bavarian Forest into play. The log raft was tied onto the boat and floated easily behind it to the center of the lake. Klaus tied the boat up to the raft, then stepped aboard to drop the anchor. The raft dipped, then moved forward until he cinched up the anchor rope, then he stepped back into the boat. The raft was not as steady as he had hoped.

"And that is a task the Americans think you need three men to handle? I came out here for this?"

"No, Obersturmführer, you came to observe the bombing, right?"

"I hope it will yield more information than our little boat ride."

"Oh, it will. You are going to get to see skip bombing from the enemy's viewpoint, on deck looking right into the bomber's cockpit. The best seat in the house."

"What stupidity are you spouting, Private Lang?"

"I mean you're going to be right here in the Bavarian Forest when the bombs come skipping across the water."

"What—you're crazy!" Von Hoffmann stood in the boat and yelled, "Help! Get me off this boat! Now!" Wagner grabbed von Hoffmann and slammed him back into a seated position. Klaus moved closely to him and placed a butcher's knife to his throat.

"Remember those missing utensils from the kitchen? One seems to have come on our *little boat ride* tonight." Klaus pressed the tip against von Hoffmann's throat. "Yell again and I'll kill you. Take off your clothes!"

"You're crazy. They'll hang you, killing a German officer. If the Americans don't, our army will."

"Clothes!" Von Hoffmann made no move, so Klaus began unbuttoning his shirt. The lieutenant kicked at him. In return, Klaus nicked his throat; a small trickle ran to his chest. Klaus wiped it away with the shirt.

"Can't have blood in the boat, Wagner." Klaus had unbuckled von Hoffmann's pants, then untied his shoes. Now when he kicked, Wagner simply pressured his arms to the breaking point. Removal of pants, shoes, undershorts left the now frightened von Hoffmann pleading for mercy.

"Why are you doing this? Are you going to drown me?"

"No, in fact we're not going to kill you or even hurt you, unless you don't cooperate."

"Then what are you doing?"

"We're leaving you. You're finally going to experience combat as we have, little man. When you spit on the Afrika Korps and beat our men in their beds, did you think we would take it forever?"

Klaus began to wrap von Hoffmann's ankles together with silver duct tape.

"Stand him up!"

Wagner stood the SS man onto his feet. They both teetered as the small boat rocked from side to side.

"Now turn him around." Von Hoffmann lost his balance, falling toward the lake side of the boat

"I've got him!" Wagner said between gritted teeth, attempting to speak as softly as possible.

Klaus secured the tape around von Hoffmann's wrists, then his arms to his body.

Von Hoffmann screamed, in English, "Help, help, there is murder here!"

"Scream again and I'll tape your mouth."

"Do it anyway, Klaus, he's not going to go quietly."

Klaus taped the man's mouth and around to the back of his head.

"Did you know, von swine, that sometimes a British fighter plane would skip a bomb across the sand to hit a tank? It's quite a sight to see, like a bowling ball bearing down on the pins—and now you get to see it for yourself."

Wagner pushed himself from the side of the boat and onto the raft. His two hundred and fifty pounds rocked the raft dangerously. Klaus held von Hoffmann and tried to establish a steady base to help lift him onto the raft.

"What ever happened to Obersturmführer von Hoffmann?"

"Ahh, mein Führer, didn't you hear? He felt so guilty of crimes against defenseless people he went to pieces in the Bavarian Forest."

"Shut up and stop gloating, Klaus. We haven't done this yet. Get him closer so I can pull him on the raft." Klaus moved the SS man to the side of the boat where Wagner grabbed him under an armpit and pulled. The raft tilted with von Hoffmann's weight and von Hoffmann's legs slid into the water.

"Careful!" hissed Klaus.

"Why not drown him, weigh him down and drop him," said Wagner, as he struggled with balance and controlling the wide-eyed man.

"Because the divers will scour the bottom of the lake in a few days looking for unexploded bombs and would find the body. Besides, Werner would miss all the fireworks. Can't deny you that, can we, Obersturmführer?"

Wagner had now pulled the taped man onto the raft, where he lay writhing and trying to speak. From a kneeling position, he dragged him to the base of one of the timbers. He lifted von Hoffmann on his shoulder as he did a balancing dance to the precarious rocking of the Forest.

"I can't hold him up and tape him as well. Take the boat and go around to the other side, it will help balance the raft, and we can both tape him to the log." Klaus marveled at Wagner's calm under pressure. He did as he was told. His weight did help right the tilting logs to a better place, though the combined weight of Wagner and von Hoffmann still presented a problem. Wagner now had von Hoffmann standing and pinned against a timber. Von Hoffmann shook his head and screamed against the tape.

Klaus began wrapping him, going around and around the log in an almost frenzied manner. Von Hoffmann's body stood powerless, his frantic eyes searching the lake for some manner of rescue.

"Enough, Klaus. He's not going anywhere—at least not for a few minutes." Wagner laughed. He was enjoying this.

"You have a strange sense of humor, Wagner. I think the wrong man here was SS."

Klaus quickly motored the boat to pick up Wagner. He shined the small boat light on the naked man.

"Auf Wiedersehen, Obersturmführer. Think of it this way. If the bomb misses you will be freed and we will go to prison. If it hits—Himmler will miss you."

Klaus gunned the boat to the shore while Wagner bagged von Hoffmann's clothes and shoes.

"Don't leave anything in the boat. Did you get his tags?"

"Yes."

"Bury them deep, Wagner, but *bury* them. Don't be caught with the Obersturmführer's clothing. When you finish digging, bury the knife with the clothes. You have done well tonight. When you make your way through the fields and hear the explosions, know that one of them will be the end of this swine."

"That will be good."

"You have enough food for a day, right?"

"*Ja.*"

"They should pick you up by then. Go over your story as you walk tonight. It must be the same as mine. Do you have any regrets about tonight?"

"I thought you knew what kind of man I am."

"A brave one, that's all I care."

Klaus ran the boat up onto shore and Wagner leaped to the muddy bank, waved the sack, and disappeared. At that moment the siren went off and a voice boomed out across the lake. "All personnel clear the target area. Fifteen minutes—clear all areas. Bombing will commence in fifteen minutes!"

Klaus sped across the lake to the filtration end, ran the craft up on shore as far as he could gun it, got out and pushed it farther up. He had not docked in his designated spot, not wanting to be seen coming ashore alone. He made his way to the tower, trying to put out of his mind the possible scenarios of a failed murder. *Murder,* he hadn't thought of the word before, but though he had killed, he had never *murdered* a man. As they planned it, there had been the comforting thought that Wagner had done both.

Klaus climbed to the tower hill. A dozen men, mostly Air Force personnel, were making their way there as well. Klaus tried to mingle in and avoid any conversation with Hortz, who would surely ask about Wagner and von Hoffmann.

The next hour seemed to float by, refusing to hurry, determined to outlast Klaus Lang's sanity. *Is the "greater good" a flawed concept, as Otto had said, or is there other justification here? Strange, the killing on the battlefield that becomes routine, a hundred lives lost in a day and we take pause at the end of this one. What would Otto's Kafka have to say?*

One strike after another was called out by the wing commander, explosions echoed off the sides of the lake wall depressions, and cheers were emitted by the spectators as the extent of the damages was relayed to those without binoculars. Klaus could hear Major Nichols's comments to the attack planes as to the accuracy of their drops and resulting destruction. The Bavarian Forest was last. Klaus's tension became near panic when the plane made a run over the Forest and did not release its payload. Had they seen von Hoffmann!

"Damn it!" the major said. "You might not get two chances in combat, Patterson! Yes, make another run and drop those damn bombs! Two hundred feet, no higher, two hundred feet!"

Klaus could see only a dark spot in the lake, but the green lights were visible. The plane dove. One, two, then three explosions rang out. There was but a brief silence, then an excited wing commander yelled, "Beautiful, Patterson. I think all three were hits. Nothing but a bunch of splinters. Excellent!"

Klaus sank to a sitting position and let out his trapped breath. First step done. Now we have to get away with it.

Chapter 34

LUCK SEEMED TO STILL be on Klaus's side. That evening, the prisoners working at the lake were returned to the compound without a check of names or numbers. Hortz had looked at him strangely on the ride back but had said nothing. A guard rode with them. Klaus, though he had worked with him for several months now, was unclear as to where Hortz's loyalties might lie. At least he had made no effort to report the missing of two men that evening.

The good fortune remained with him the next morning as he, Hortz, and the two men who had ridden in Hortz's boat boarded a work truck that carried prisoners to their jobs. Though it was Saturday, the cleanup would proceed. He was puzzled, though much relieved, that he hadn't been called in to explain the disappearance of the two men who certainly must be missed by now. At the lake, the American sergeant who was their bombing range overseer outlined the workday which would consist of removing any target remains that hadn't sunk to the bottom. Klaus had hoped to go out in his boat alone, but he had been paired with a Private Wilheim, a sad-eyed young man in his twenties who had worked with Hortz the night before.

Klaus boated to the docks first. At each, they dragged wood to the side and stacked it for burning. At Dock Pepper, Klaus told Wilheim to continue there and he would go to the Bavarian Forest to see if there were pieces that would have to be towed ashore rather than put in the boat. Wilheim just nodded and continued his work.

The exact location of where the target had been anchored was somewhat in question. Shards of timber floated about, but Klaus was amazed at the total destruction of the timber target, not one intact log remained. A faint smell of explosives remained in the area. He began to load small pieces into the boat when he saw duct tape on one of the scraps. He picked it up and gasped. There was a piece of flesh still stuck to the tape! It had not sunk because of the floating wood. Klaus motored about the site, picking up five more grisly pieces. He put them in a sack, though they would have sunk when freed from the wood that floated them. Klaus tossed in more wood, feeling somewhat sure that no more parts of von Hoffmann remained afloat.

When he returned to the dock, he began unloading his wood. He tossed the sack on the pile and covered it with wood.

"What's in the sack?" asked Wilheim.

"We had to tape a couple of the logs together and some of the duct tape was still floating around. Thought we'd just burn it with the wood."

Yes, Werner von Hoffmann, you will get a warm-up toast before you burn in hell.

Chapter 35

KLAUS AND YOUNG WILHEIM continued to stack the exploded dock wood for burning.

"We burn?"

"No, too wet, Wilheim. I'll come back and do it next week." Klaus continued to pile wood, completely obscuring the sack, the pieces he piled on too heavy for an animal to burrow through to get at the sack. At least that was his hope. He must make sure of that, then risk another run to get Forest wood. Klaus worked with a nervous energy, aware that it wasn't over yet. He had seen a jeep bouncing around the lake, coming in their direction.

A lone MP, armed, wearing a thick plastic duty helmet and sunglasses, approached in the jeep. He called out, "POW Lang! Prisoner Lang!" He stopped before the two men.

"Yes, that's me, "said Klaus.

"Hop in, you're going with me."

"Where?"

"To the base. Lieutenant Wills wants to ask you some questions."

Klaus climbed in.

"No need to take the boat out again, Wilheim. Just stack the stuff near the shore. I'll do the rest Monday." Wilheim didn't answer.

Lieutenant Wills awaited him in the guard's office of the stockade.

"I told them to pull you before you went out on work detail today."

"Sorry, sir. We left early."

"All right, Private Lang. I'll get right down to it. What happened with Wagner and von Hoffmann last night?"

"Von Hoffmann wanted to leave …"

"Escape?"

"Yes, I suppose so. He just said 'I'm leaving,' and left."

"And Wagner?"

"It was almost like he hadn't thought of it and said to himself, *Ja, I think I'll go, too.* Neither man had ever been outside the compound or base. I guess it was too tempting."

"And you didn't report their leaving?"

"Not my responsibility, I'm not a guard. I only account for Klaus Lang."

"You don't know where they were going?"

"They didn't share that with me."

"Just so you know, we caught Wagner about an hour ago, just strolling along, eating a bratwurst like he didn't have a care in the world."

"Too bad, but you know, Lieutenant, Wagner is not a bright man. I doubt he had a grand plan. Did you catch von Hoffmann as well?"

"Not yet—he couldn't have gotten far, they never do."

"Well, von Hoffmann is not Wagner, sir. He's a dangerous, clever man."

"You just don't disappear in this open farm land."

"Not exactly the Bavarian Forest, is it, Lieutenant?" Klaus bit his lip. Stupid! Stupid! Lieutenant Wills seemed not to hear.

"Doesn't matter anyway, Lang. Orders came in yesterday to transfer von Hoffmann to Alva. Soon as we catch him, he's headed for the camp with his SS buddies."

Klaus closed his eyes and sat back slowly into the chair.

Chapter 36

OTTO LAY IN HIS bunk in a state of sleep which seemed not like sleep at all but *memory* that he could steer in any direction, select any subject and it would be real, so alive he could reach out and touch it. It was always the same; he walked with Margret and Lorenz through the garden city, along the Elbe to the crown gate of the Palace. They each held his hand and answered the continuous questioning of a bright and curious young boy. They told him he would someday go to his father's school and he could be a physician like his grandfather or a teacher like his father. He would be tall and strong, and his friends would be the same. Then suddenly they would be walking in a wadi in Tunisia among the blooming almond trees and esparto grass.

Otto wanted to stay in Dresden, but he was never able to end the dream there. Margret and Lorenz walked ahead of him in the wadi and he could not close the distance between them. He called out their names, but they did not turn to him. Soon he could see them no more.

At that point, Otto's sleep would become fitful, the dream would turn to questions that were with him every waking hour. What if the absence of mail has a tragic answer? Could he go on without his family? Zimmerman's wild eyes and screams came back to him, jarring him to a sitting position on his sweat-soaked bed.

Chapter 37

THE SKIES HAD BEEN cloudy of late, and rain was predicted to fall once again in an uncommonly wet August for West Texas. The billowy white clouds would give way to a dark storm mass that could form suddenly on the plain. Some protection from the sun's rays was the clouds' gift; the price, a humidity that was smothering.

Otto and Klaus, who were once again able to talk and dine together, sat on chairs outside the barracks awaiting the dinner hour. Klaus held the floor in a mesmerizing account of last Friday's disposal of Obersturmführer von Hoffmann.

"You must not share any of this, Otto, even with Hans."

"I understand that. And the word on Wagner?"

"He's doing five days in the stockade," Klaus laughed. "Five days for a man who spent five years in Landsberg Prison. It's like having to stand in the corner in kindergarten."

"Do you think he told Lieutenant Wills the correct story?"

"I trust Wagner. All he had to do was convince Wills that von Hoffmann had civilian clothes and a bag hidden by the lake. The most important part of the story was that von Hoffmann told him he could not go with him because there was *only room* for one man."

"So Wills is to think someone was waiting to pick up von Hoffmann in a vehicle of some sort?"

"The only way to explain his complete vanishing."

"And how sure are you that the divers won't find pieces of our little man?"

"They're looking for *bombs*, bombs only. They can't be concerned with debris on the lake bottom. Tomorrow I will go burn the wood, if I'm allowed to go back on the team."

"Why wouldn't you be?"

"They're upset I just let the two men go."

"You're not a guard!"

"That's what I told them."

"I have guilt for letting you do my job but admiration for your plan, Klaus!"

"Wagner was the key. If I hadn't had him, my so-called *plan* would have been kaputt. The man is a *bulle*."

"Come, let's go eat and visit Hans."

"Hans is not to know, no one is to know."

"I told you I understand that, Klaus."

"One more thing I must share, Otto. Von Hoffmann had orders to be transferred to Alva. The order arrived Friday."

"Alva!" Otto gasped. "He was going to Alva?" Then he smiled. "I find great humor in that."

"I'm not sorry. We created room on the earth, one clean, new space."

"*Ja, ja*, he was an animal who needed to be put down. You should *never* feel regret, Klaus."

Hans greeted them warmly, foregoing the wurst routine for a long handshake that said everything.

"What's for dinner, my friend?"

"Pork chops!"

"Ahh, poor Kumpel, probably one of his piggy friends."

When Hans joined them at their table, there were no questions asked about von Hoffmann's escape or Wagner's internment. Perhaps Hans had come to his own conclusions.

"And your escape, Klaus, is that still on?"

"Yes, it will be soon if we get the rains that are forecast. Escape in the rain negates the dogs following us. Also, if you'll remember the last heavy rains, the electricity went out and they had to go to the big generator. We have a man who will disable the generator the day or so before the escape. Then we will short the main electricity just before we leave."

"How many men, Klaus?" asked Otto.

"Over twenty. That may increase when we cut through the fences. Sorry to disparage the camp builders, Herr Otto, but this isn't a very secure prison. Getting out is the easy part."

"Twenty men! That will be chaos."

"Only about five of us are serious, Otto. The others see it as some sort of holiday. I have money, clothes, I have papers, and best of all, I speak the language. Once on the outside, we will go in four directions. I will proceed to Mexico; some will try for the West Coast, Canada, the East. Think of the turmoil, the confusion. Give us a few days and we will be in so many states and countries they'll never find us. If we're caught, what? The stockade—what is there to lose?"

"Your life, maybe," said Hans. "Some trigger-happy guard or cowboy. Some hunter who would like to mount your head alongside his buffalo and bighorn sheep."

"Thank you for your encouragement, Hans."

"Why don't you go with us, Otto? You have all the advantages I have, plus you're smarter."

"No, I won't be going with you."

"Aw, Crazy Otto, the Americans will be so disappointed, their favorite runner passing up the party."

"I wish you well, Klaus. I might not see you until after the war."

"Or the day after the escape. Whichever comes first."

"I believe you will do well, my friend. Don't hurt anyone, civilian or soldier. The stockade is one thing, hanging is another."

"I will take your advice, Private Becker, as always."

Chapter 38

THE RAIN FELL HEAVIER now. The faded asphalt roof of the farmhouse turned away the downpour that pinged on the barn's tin cover like a drumline using chopsticks. The lightning turned horizontal at times, one strike following another. While the boy awaited Mr. Mac's return from town, the storm had brought with it an early darkness. J.T. had tried the lights but there were none, so he felt his way to the matches Mr. Mac kept near the fireplace. He was able to find the kerosene lamp and light it. He went to the phone to call his mama, but it was dead, as well. He must make a decision: wait here for Mr. Mac or try to get to the base with the empty barrels. He could leave the truck there and catch the last bus to town, then return by bus in the morning to pick up the truck and the filled slop barrels.

He started the truck motor with some trepidation. He had never driven in bad weather and he doubted his ability to navigate the muddy road to the highway, but he didn't want to stay in the eerie farmhouse watching the lamplight flicker its beams across the empty kitchen. He'd rather walk than stay there. Farmer Mac always seemed reluctant to have him inside the house, as if the memories there were his only and visitors could not share them.

The wheels were already slipping, the ruts swerving him from one side of the road to the other. A coyote ran in front of his headlights, startling him. He veered near the ditch but righted the old truck in time. *Got to hunt, even in bad weather,* he thought. *Actually probably easier to creep up on a rabbit. Can rabbits smell coyotes in the rain? Pay attention to your driving, J.T., don't have to tell Mama tomorrow you ran the truck in a ditch.* Even in the darkness he knew he must be getting close to the highway. The windshield wipers were of little help, one having only half rubber, the metal half scraping loudly on the windshield on each labored sweep.

He could see what he thought was the highway about a half mile ahead, and his confidence grew. Once on the asphalt, his driving would cease to be cretin and his chances of breaking down as slim as getting an A in algebra. There was a knocking from the back of the truck, a new noise among the dozens the old truck gave off normally. He couldn't place it, then heard it again. He looked back in the cab's rear window and he saw a face. Mr. Becker! He skidded forward another fifty yards, then stopped.

Otto, every inch of him drenched, opened the passenger door of the truck and climbed in. He was wearing civilian clothing.

"Mr. Becker, what are you doing here?"

"I was hidden in the back of your truck, taking in the aroma of rotting food."

"You missed the truck back to camp?"

"Yes, on purpose, Kumpel. I am going to escape the prison."

"Escape?"

"Yes."

"Won't they miss you and come lookin' for you?"

"Maybe not tonight. There will be such confusion there, I doubt they will know I'm gone."

"I wish you wouldn't, Mr. Becker. They might shoot you or something bad like that."

"I've been shot before, it wouldn't be a new experience. You must not waste your worry on me."

"But you're my friend, Mr. Becker."

"Yes, that is true, but you must save your concern for your brother and your country. I have told you that. The enemy is still the enemy, at least this day. Another day …"

"It's hard, Mr. Becker."

"Yes, it's hard. I hope you never have to go to war, Kumpel."

"Where're you going?"

"Away, Kumpel, away. You will probably never see me again," said Otto.

"If I'm caught, they will likely transfer me because I have two escapes. If they don't, I will request transfer. One way or another, my days at Camp 67 are at an end."

J.T. did not speak. Otto took his identity tag from around his neck, broke it in half, and gave the unattached part to J.T.

"Here, keep this and you will remember our good days together, not our parting."

"I will, sir, and I'll *never* forget you."

"And take this medal. It is called an Iron Cross and it's worth a good deal of money. Sell it and buy your clothes and, of course, Charles Atlas."

"I couldn't take that, sir."

"Yes, you can. If I'm caught, they will take it from me anyway. I don't need the medal, I have the memory.

"You have become a man, Kumpel. It has been my pleasure to see you grow up, in one summer, now a man. You are an innocent who has been chosen."

"For what, sir?"

"To be Jerome Thayer Graham and for all to see your example."

"I never understand you, Mr. Becker."

"I must go now. Please give me the keys to the truck."

"You want the truck!"

"Yes."

"It doesn't have much gas."

"Yes it does, I filled it. I also put two gas cans in the back, and I have gas stamps."

J.T. was stunned. He sat motionless.

"The keys, Kumpel. I must hasten on."

J.T. took the keys out of the ignition but held them tightly in his hand.

"Would you kill me if I didn't give them to you?"

Otto looked at the boy, tears welling up in both their eyes. *If there is a God, let my son grow up to be like this boy, this young **man**,* he thought.

"No, I would never harm you, Kumpel." Otto opened his door. "I will walk."

J.T. stretched out his arm toward Otto, palm up with the keys resting there. Otto took the keys and exited the truck cab and came to the driver's side. J.T. was standing there. Otto took him in his arms and held him tightly.

"Auf Wiedersehen, my dear Kumpel."

"Goodbye, Mr. Becker. Good luck."

J.T. stood in the rain watching as the truck's lights were finally extinguished by the elements. He began to walk back toward the farm, the sucking ooze of his boots pulling from the mud the only sound. The rain came in sheets now, mixing with his tears, a taste of salt and sadness. He thought of what he would tell Mr. Mac if he had returned home. It must be the truth, he knew that. At least he could walk back slowly, and that is what he did.

Mr. Mac's pickup was near the barn and J.T. could see several lighted lamps in the kitchen and living room. Huge puddles filled the barnyard, while small ditches formed, running the water to low spots to collect there.

J.T. pulled off his boots on the porch, knocked, and entered the house.

"What the hell ..." said Mr. Mac. "Where you been?"

"I was gonna take the truck to the base and ..."

"So you're stuck on the road, huh?"

"No, sir."

"Then where's the truck?"

"Mr. Becker took it, sir."

"The prisoner Becker?"

"Yes, sir."

"I'll be damned. Just *took* it, you say?"

"Yes, sir."

"Well he won't get far, no gas."

"He has gas, sir."

"Yeah, well he has a fifteen-year-old truck, too. He won't get far in that ole bucket of bolts."

"Yes, sir."

"You been crying?"

"I think it's just the rain, sir."

"Well, the rain made your eyes red.

"Don't worry about the truck, I ain't. Leastwise he didn't hurt you."

"Mr. Becker would never do that, sir."

"Oh yeah, he's a Nazi, ain't he?"

"No, sir, he's not."

"I ain't going back to town in this weather. You bed down here and in the morning we'll go report it to the sheriff and I'll talk to your mama." J.T. didn't answer.

"Where do you think he was goin', J.T.?"

"I think he went out for a beer."

The End

Story Fragments

•••••Approximately 440,000 enemy prisoners were held in the United States between 1942 and 1945. Of that number, 378,000 were German, 51,455 were Italian, and 5,435 were Japanese.

In addition, 110,000 Japanese Americans were sent to relocation camps, almost the entire population of that designation who lived on the West Coast. Only 1 percent of the Japanese Americans living in Hawaii were interred.

Japanese prisoners were not sent to the U.S. in great numbers. Most refused to surrender and indeed were still being captured in island jungles into the 1980s. Those held in the U.S. were treated humanely but differently. They were not allowed to work outside their compounds. As a result of the ugly treatment of Allied prisoners by their armies, the Japanese POW camps in America could never be called the Asian equivalent of the "Fritz Ritz."

•••••Whatever harsh conditions enemy prisoners endured during their internment in the USA, whether it be weather, locale, their own Nazi oppressors, or other *hardships,* they were infinitely better off than WWII prisoners held in other countries and locales. In comparison, a large number of prisoners held by the Russian and Japanese never returned, either dying or, in the case of some prisoners held by the Russians, never released.

•••••Most prison camps in the U.S. were located in the South and Southwest. Land was available there, and the right kind of land as well, isolated from major urban areas by great distances, surrounded by terrain that made escape difficult. Economically, camps in these areas were less costly to the U.S. government, the primary savings being in heating fuel. Agriculture and lumber were the predominant engines that drove these local economies. Prisoners' work in the fields and forests proved to be a major component in maintaining industries whose workers were away in the military of their country.

•••••A few prisoners were held in camps in the Northeast. There, life in some ways was more difficult than that experienced by their southern counterparts. Harsh weather, bears, fierce black flies, and mosquitoes had to be dealt with daily while those who attempted to escape faced the French Canadian mountain folk who hated Germans like no other.

•••••There were 2,222 recorded escapes during the '42-'45 period. Given the almost half million prisoners held, the percentage of attempts was lower than that of the regular U.S. prisons. Escaping was not extremely difficult, but *staying free* was. The majority of escapees were caught within hours or days. As mentioned, the location of the POW camp usually played a role in their capture. The prisoner in the southeast had to contend with the swamps, rugged wooded areas, and law enforcement officers highly experienced in tracking criminals through its dangerous terrain.

•••••In many recorded cases, citizens either assisted in the recapture of POW escapees or captured them themselves. There were isolated exceptions. One American soldier helped POWs escape. He was sentenced to death but President Roosevelt later commuted his sentence. Two Japanese American girls became romantically involved with two Italian POWs and helped in their escape. They were sentenced to two years in prison.

•••••477 POWs died during their stay in U.S. compounds: 265 died of natural causes, 72 by suicide, and 56 were shot to death during some part of their escape. Others died victims of the elements while escaping; others are listed in a miscellaneous category.

In 1945, 14 German prisoners were added to those numbers when they were executed at the U.S. Disciplinary Barracks, Fort Leavenworth, Kansas. They had been sentenced to death for killing three of their fellow prisoners caught collaborating with their American keepers. President Truman declined to give the men clemency.

•••••In retrospect, it is believed by a number of historians that Eisenhower's drop of safe conduct passes over and behind German lines worked. The promise of "the good life" was said to have contributed to a large number of surrenders.

•••••There were several motivations that drove POWs in America to try to escape. Among them were:

Hope to actually make it to a port city and stow away on a ship to Europe.

The rumor that South American countries were sympathetic to the German cause and would provide them sanctuary. No POWs were able to test that theory, but the post-war years found many German military men, including Nazis, making their way to Brazil and Argentina where they became citizens or favored guests.

With papers appearing to be authentic, some sought to blend in with Americans and remain undetected. This worked for several prisoners who remained at large for half a dozen years. These escapees met the most important prerequisite of successful escape: they spoke excellent English.

Some prisoners escaped as a lark, a game to see how long they could outwit their captors; others wanted to experience a feeling of freedom even if it were a brief one. Boredom, depression as they contemplated years more of being locked away, were frequently cited reasons given by prisoners after they were captured. The hope of meeting a woman was a powerful urge that drove many to flight.

•••••A prisoner named Fritz Dreschler escaped for fairly long periods, not once but *three* times. He became known as the *Escape King of Florida.*

•••••Johan Klapper fashioned his own version of escape. He sought flight not from his captors but from the pressures and brutality present in the barracks where he lived. Johan dug a hole under a building on the Army base and took residence there. He lived in the dugout hole 95 days, foraging food in the mess hall waste bins and drinking water that dripped from an ice box in the building and seeped through cracks near Johan's nest.

•••••At the end of the war, 95,532 American soldiers were being held prisoners by the Germans.

•••••All prisoners held by the U.S. were returned to their home country in 1945. None were allowed to stay, though many petitioned to do so. A significant number of the prisoners were diverted to France and England where they spent another two years helping rebuild the infrastructure and economy of those two nations. By 1948 all prisoners had been sent home.

Many POWs held in the U.S. eventually made their way back to the U.S. and became permanent residents and citizens.

•••••In 1951 only six POWs held in the U.S. were still at large. A *Collier's* magazine article featuring the pictures of several of the men was published. It led to a rapid capture of four of the former prisoners. One was a bookstore owner who remained free until 1953, one had become a decorator, one was located in Mexico and was allowed to stay, while the fourth suffered the considerable embarrassment of being turned in by his mother-in-law. To this date there are two prisoners for which there has never been an accounting.